AVALANCHE

by the same author

Below the Horizon
The Sea Above Them
Oil Strike

AVALANCHE

John Wingate

St. Martin's Press
New York

Library of Congress Cataloging in Publication Data
Wingate, John.
  Avalanche.
  I. Title.
PZ4.W7667Av3 [PR6073.I53] 823'.9'14 76–54635

All characters in this book are entirely
fictitious but, if anyone should recognize
his or herself, the fact is entirely coincidental
and I offer my apologies.

To K and John
with affection and gratitude

Acknowledgements

I am very grateful to
L'Institut Geographique National of France
for the friendly help which was given me in the preparation
of this book.
My thanks are due also to Mr Colin Fraser
whom regretfully I have never met, for having written his
fascinating and authoritative book, *The Avalanche Enigma*
(John Murray) to which I made frequent reference.
I thank also The Ski Club of Great Britain
which gave me good advice.

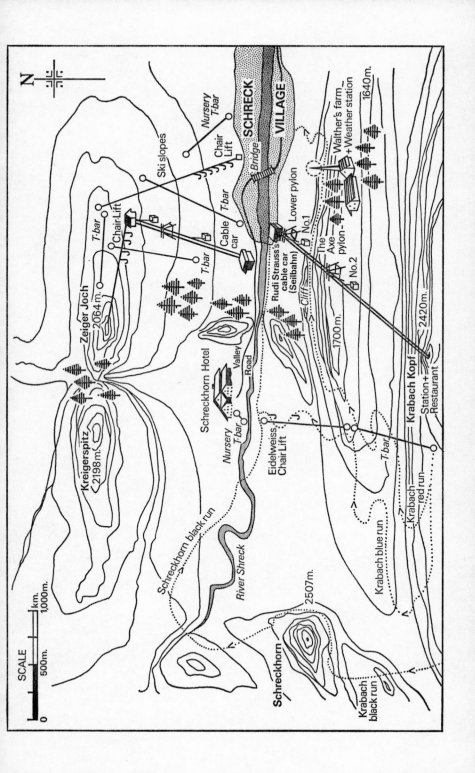

Chapter 1

'You're wanted in the Telex room, Mr Trevallack.'

Dirk Trevallack, Assistant Manager of British Bank (Middle East), Beirut, continued for a moment checking the register. Mrs Kim Quintan's self-satisfied attitude always irritated him – and particularly so this morning after his late night checking of the codes. The 'stand-by' from London came through yesterday – and today was Christmas Eve. A choice moment to pick for the monthly panic.

'Mr Trevallack . . .'

He rose impatiently from his desk. Kim Quintan was on form this morning. He glanced at the image looking back at him from the long mirrors on the ornate, hand-forged grille-work of the double doors that led from the main hall. BB was one of the most staid of Lebanon's banks, and its dignified decor emphasized its stability in these troubled times. He was not used to his new rimless spectacles; and he still resented, profoundly, the blow that had struck him so suddenly when he had been training with the commandos on the assault course at Topsham. He had been unable to see the bull when he had come on target with his rifle. For two days he had kept the secret to himself. He had been forced to report to the MO because, when cliff-scaling, he was becoming a menace to the others. So they had chucked him out of the Royal Marines. Apart from wearing his spectacles, nothing could be done for his eyesight which had dropped below the standards set by the Service.

'Maria is waiting, Mr Trevallack.'

Damn the officious Mrs Quintan. He hitched up his black-and-white chequered trousers, smoothed back his groomed, black hair and slicked his military moustache with the back of his forefinger. His tired brown eyes and the circles beneath them emphasized the greyness of his face which was beginning to betray the soft living he was enjoying here. Still, for twenty-nine, he was wearing well enough. More skiing was what he needed, on the slopes behind Qarnt es Sude, up at three thousand metres. Though he was over six-foot-two, he could compete with most of his Lebanese friends. He could certainly out-ski Kim Quintan, thank God, though she was a ski-tourer, a *langlauf* maniac. He was putting on weight and he tucked the blue short-sleeved shirt into his flared trousers. These modern buildings were too warm, but oil came cheaper out here, so near to the sheik tycoons.

'Well, Kim, what's all the panic about?'

He enjoyed calling her by her Christian name, as he addressed all the girls in the bank. She resented his approach and persisted in her formality.

'No panic, Mr Trevallack, but London seems to be in a hurry.'

He glanced at the telex. The machine was purring impatiently, waiting for its orders.

'*Information received coup imminent stop Execute Operation Oedipus.*'

For an instant, he remained staring at the top priority message from St Swithin's Mews, the Bank's International Head Office in London. There was no doubt about it – and Thompson, the manager here in Beirut, was down in Cairo, negotiating for a new office in that city which had become so important with the re-opened canal. No dodging this one. He, Dirk Trevallack, had his orders. He looked up and met the smirk of amusement on Kim Quintan's face. The green-flecked hazel eyes did not conceal her contempt at his hesitancy. He had shot too much of a line sometimes: the esteem which a Royal Marine officer felt for the Corps was not necessarily shared by a female bank clerk.

'I'll leave at once, Kim. I'd like you to come with me. I need your knowledge of the language.' He saw the surprise in her eyes, but she would not admit her distaste for the disturbance in routine.

'I'll come,' she said. 'Can you give me ten minutes to collect my things?'

'Okay. I'll pick up the codes and collect the cash. Meet me in the strongroom at 10.30.'

She had already turned away and was picking up her handbag from her desk. He followed her out and crossed directly to the Chief Clerk's office.

'I'm leaving you in charge, Mr Mefsut. I'll be away for a few days. I'm taking Mrs Quintan with me.'

Mefsut was a good friend and no fool. He raised his black eyebrows, his intelligent eyes asking no questions. He did not even demand the keys of the strongroom.

'Get through to Mr Thompson. Tell him we've received OEDIPUS. I'll leave enough cash in the safe for today's business.'

Mefsut rose from his chair. He shook Trevallack's hand and accompanied the Cornishman to the doorway. 'Allah be with you, Dirk,' he said. 'Take care.'

Dirk Trevallack admired the courage of these men. In the cross-fire of Lebanon's tragic politics, those who worked for the foreigners often went in fear of their lives. He closed Mefsut's door behind him and went down to the basement garage where he left his 304 Peugeot brake. Yesterday he had bought six jerrycans and stuffed them surreptitiously in the back. He would fill up with petrol as soon as he was clear of the town.

He picked up the haversacks, one with emergency rations and the bedroll, the other empty. Quietly he made his way back to the rear staircase. He paused a moment outside the cedar door, then strolled down the passage towards the strongroom. He met no one and swiftly entered the barred room, turning his key in the lock. He closed the inner door behind him, so that he could work unobserved.

Stupid, wasn't it, how excitement sharpened the nerves? He worked swiftly, gathering up the sealed, brown envelopes which he had prepared yesterday. These were the vital authentication tables, codes and cables by which the bank conducted its international business. Through their secrecy, millions of pounds' worth of business was transacted daily. If these documents were compromised by falling into unauthorized hands, the whole of the bank's network would be jeopardized. London had been specific: the British Consul in Ankara was alerted to receive the precious codes. Trevallack had been authorized to take with him as much cash in foreign currencies as he thought necessary for his journey.

He opened the inner safe. Yes, there it was, the small packet he had prepared with such care. Cash in Lebanese, Syrian and Turkish notes; his American Express card and the cheques; the Eurocard, the dollars and the German marks. In all, he had over two thousand pounds in cash, plus the invaluable credit cards. That ought to be enough for all eventualities, even for two people – and he wondered whether his pique at selecting Kim Quintan had been a ridiculous decision . . . ? Too late now, anyway – and then he heard a gentle scratching on the door. That would be her. 10.30 already – on the dot.

'Can you manage the heavy haversack? I'll take the codes . . . it'll look better if we've a sack each.'

3

She nodded as he tucked the cash inside his shirt. Once in the car he could split the money with her and find a secure hiding place for the codes.

'Ready?'

She nodded, the beam from the bright spot-light above them catching the tints in her red hair. She was sensibly dressed in jeans, with an anorak over her arm concealing the sailing bag slung from her shoulder. He opened the door and peered outside. No one. She slipped past him and began hurrying down the passage as he slammed the safe door shut after him. He spun the combination lock, closed the grille and left the strongroom. He swung the massive door behind him and turned the lock. Mefsut had no keys, so the staff would be safe enough if the bank was raided. They had orders not to resist, if life was at risk. The cash remaining was minimal, anyway, but it hurt to leave it for the taking . . .

Down in the garage basement, Kim Quintan was waiting by the Peugeot's locked door. He unlocked the car, slung the haversacks in the back and started up. He switched on the sidelights and drove out into the daylight. He paused on the pavement to see if the road was clear. Something was approaching from the left. He would take the avenue, then cut across round the back of the city for the Ba'albek road. Though it was longer by the mountain route, it was quicker for the Syrian border, Homs, Hama and Aleppo. Then the Turkish frontier at Raju, and they were virtually safe. To reach the Ba'albek main road, it would be quickest to cut back along the front of the bank. At the end of the avenue, he swung off to the left, then left again to the boulevard flanking the imposing array of modern office blocks.

This was one of his favourite routes in this beautiful city. The lines of acacia and gently swaying palms lent an air of eastern mystery to the concrete monuments of modern living bordering the central flower beds which ran down the middle of the boulevard. He took the Peugeot steadily down the right-hand lane, then slowed as a blockage in the traffic ahead brought him to a halt.

'Look there, Mr Trevallack . . .'

He followed Kim's pointing finger. On the opposite side of the boulevard, he could glimpse through the palm trees a jammed morass of traffic. Horns were blaring – nothing out of the ordinary for Beirut – but what was unusual were the running men cordoning off the area. They were masked in gangster style, grotesque in their

4

stocking hoods, as they waved their automatic weapons in spiralling circles.

As the traffic on Dirk's side began to stream ahead, he realized suddenly that he was driving past his bank. He took his eyes off the road momentarily, and there it was, *British Bank* (Beirut), in its bold but restrained letters of black and gold. In the portals through which he had passed daily for over two years, several bandits were standing guard. From the shadows inside, a plume of smoke emerged. He heard a muffled bang, felt a pressure on his ears, then caught the sound of breaking glass. He put his foot down and let the Peugeot have her head.

He had never driven so recklessly before in this city. He lane-hopped to the end of the boulevard, then swung off to the Ba'albek road. From the corner of his eye he could see Kim Quintan's hand gripping the edge of her seat. She remained calm, but was turning her head to peer through the rear window. They drove on in silence until he reached the junction. He swooped into the Shell filling station.

' 'Morning, Mr Trevallack.'

'Tank up, Joe . . . and these jerrycans, please.'

They jumped out. 'Get some food,' Dirk whispered. 'Anything you like. I shan't stop until we're in Turkey.'

Mrs Quintan hurried across to the self-service at the end of the garage. Dirk re-stowed the gear, taking the code-haversack into the front, where he shoved it beneath his driving seat. He found a spanner in the tool-kit and tucked it next to the hand-brake. There was no other weapon.

'Thanks, Joe. Keep the change.'

The grinning attendant finished wiping off the dust from the windscreen as Kim returned hurriedly, her arms laden.

'You'll be sick of boiled sweets by the time the day's over,' she said, 'and I've plenty of fruit.'

'All set?' He watched her slipping the belt about her, then let in the clutch. Oil okay, full of juice, tyres fixed yesterday – and the road stretching out before them. They were away, but he could not help but wonder what devilment was going on at the bank. The *coup d'état* had been expected, but whether it was the communists or the military junta was anybody's guess. He slipped into top gear. The brake began purring along the arterial road leading into Syria through the mountain range. He could see the snow even now, white-capped peaks, like icing on a cake. The gradient was increasing and he slipped her down to third: the jerrycans weighed more than he thought.

'You okay, Kim?'

Mrs Quintan was turning round and was peering over the seat into the recesses of the brake. The road was curling upwards now, snaking through the valley separating the twin peaks of Qarnt es Sude and Halimet el Qabu. Their summits were piercing the grey wisps of cloud drifting across the ranges. In less than an hour at this rate he would be passing between them.

'Mr Trevallack?'

'Yes?'

The woman was peering out of her window and looking down upon the snaking bends they had negotiated minutes earlier.

'I didn't mention it before, because I didn't want to worry you . . .'

'Yes, what's up?'

'I've been watching them now for some while. We're being followed, Mr Trevallack. Two cars and they've blue flashing lights.'

Chapter 2

Dirk kept his foot down and they reached the outskirts of Ba'albek at noon. The Peugeot behaved impeccably and appeared to draw ahead of the cars trailing some eight kilometres behind. Occasionally Kim would catch sight of one of them as the road wound up the valley, but, if nothing untoward happened, Dirk ought to reach the Syrian frontier ahead of their pursuers. Relations between the Lebanon and Syria, as tragic as ever, were particularly strained at the moment and, with today's *coup d'état*, would be even more so. Dirk said nothing, but he sensed that his thoughts reflected those of the silent woman beside him. If the Lebanese had closed the frontier, Dirk had no choice other than to crash his way through the barrier. The Syrians might be delighted to help anyone wishing to escape from the civil-war-torn Lebanon.

They left Ba'albek behind them and at 12.20 the twin, snow-covered peaks drifted past them on either side. The village of Qu'a next, deserted at this hour, and then the frontier directly ahead, less than eight kilometres distant. Dirk was forcing himself to think again in kilometres – eight kilometres to the frontier post.

'Okay, Kim?' He could feel the tension between them. These frontier guards were a trigger-happy lot.

'Yes, thanks.' She was barely audible above the roar of the car's progress.

'If they start shooting, I'm going straight through.'

'Okay.'

'Keep your head down and duck beneath the panel.' He slipped his hand from the gear lever and momentarily rested his fingers on the sleeve of her forearm. 'All right, Kim?'

'Fine, Mr . . .'

'*Dirk*,' he said. 'You're more scared at calling me by my Christian name than you are of Arabs and their guns.'

She withdrew her arm. She busily fluffed up her rusty curls and stared out of her window. She was flustered, he could see from the mounting colour in her cheek. He realized then that he knew nothing about this woman. She had built such a barrier around her, that he had not bothered to penetrate it.

She was turning towards him, and from the corner of his eye he could see the strain on her face. Her compressed lips barely moved when she spoke.

'Dirk,' she said shyly. 'Thanks. I don't know why you've brought me, but I'm glad now.' She peered through the windscreen at the bend coming up ahead.

'Here it is,' she said. '*Douane*, two kilometres.'

He kept his foot down. He would not decelerate until the last second.

'Get out the map and let's have your passport,' he said. 'Keep staring at the route, while I deal with the guards. Act wet.'

'I'll be myself then.' He caught the bitterness of her short laugh as she leaned across him towards the glove compartment. She was smiling and suddenly he was glad.

Here it was – the white-washed huts on either side of the tarred road; the red and white poles of the barrier; and the Syrian *douane* a couple of hundred yards further on. He could distinguish the figure of a Lebanese guard slumped in a chair in the glass-fronted customs' hut. Keep it cool, Trevallack. They're dozy from their midday blow-out – and he could see the hands of the clock on the wall almost coming up to one o'clock. He drew up opposite the opened door of the kiosk, but left the engine running. A bleary-eyed man sporting the fashionable Mexican moustache, yawned, took the drooping cigar from his mouth and held out his hand for the passports. His companion was asleep, stretched out in the corner.

'English,' Dirk said. 'How far to Aleppo, please?'

The guard peered across at him. Momentarily his concentration was distracted, as he glanced at the road map on the opposite wall.

'Aleppo?' He scrutinized the two passports, peered sleepily first at Kim, then at Dirk. . . . 'Two hundred and ten, Mister. *Bonne route* . . .' and he handed back the passports as the radio telephone began crackling from the rack by his left shoulder. The barrier rose slowly. He waved Dirk through and plucked at the telephone.

Unhurriedly Dirk replaced the passports in the glove locker. He slipped into first, then drew slowly ahead as Kim pored over her map. He heard a shout and, peering through the rear mirror, he saw the guard waving excitedly. He was holding the R/T phone in one hand while the other was struggling with his revolver holster.

Dirk put his foot down, sounded his horn and screeched up to the Syrian barrier just as the pole lifted. Two grinning Syrians, fully alert now from the cries of their opposite numbers, held up their hands. Dirk braked hard and Kim jolted forward into her safety belt. She extricated the passports from the locker and, with a smile, handed them through Dirk's opened window.

'Good afternoon,' she said in her best Syrian. 'We are English and want to tour your beautiful country.' Dirk understood the gist of it, but he felt nervous as the volatile Syrians glanced at their passports. The two guards saluted and grinned. They nodded towards Lebanon.

'Don't like the Liban, heh?' one asked. 'Better here, in Syrie?' The man saluted and they were waved through. Thank God. . . . Dirk had been ready to bribe them both with a hundred smackers each. He let in the clutch and they were away. As he peered into the rear mirror again, he saw the Syrians jeering at their Lebanese brothers. They were waving their arms in derision, as a couple of cars with blinking blue lights drew up at the Lebanese frontier pole. He could see the blue-uniformed police jumping out and running towards the Syrians. They were gesticulating madly when Dirk's Peugeot rounded the bend.

'Forty to Homs,' Kim said. 'D'you think the Syrians'll let them through?'

Dirk did not answer as he glanced at the imperturbable Mrs Quintan. 'You did all right,' he said.

'Will they be allowed through, Dirk?' she repeated.

'Depends how they tell their story to our Syrian friends. If they present us as imperialist foreign bankers, I reckon they'll set the Syrians after us, even if they don't follow us themselves.'

They drove in silence – but at least they were through the first barrier. They swept through the village of El Qoussair, then came to a fork. 'To the right,' Kim said, 'is the main road to Homs. It's longer and I doubt if it's quicker. Straight on is direct and one side of the triangle.'

As they began to pick up speed again, two figures emerged from the scrub on the right side of the road. They looked like students, a lanky youth and his girl. They were thumbing their way north, by the look of them, trying to escape the holocaust to come. . . . The

9

terrible days of '75 and '76 were too recent for prudent citizens to forget. Dirk pulled up.

'Aleppo,' he said. 'Any good to you?'

'Thanks. Suit us fine,' the young man replied, speaking perfect American, his intelligent eyes reflecting his gratitude. He fumbled with the door that Kim had unhitched and the two scrambled in, dumping their haversacks in the rear. The smell of petrol from the jerrycans was noticeable enough, but the hitch-hikers remained silent as Dirk settled down for the long haul to Homs; twenty-five kilometres further on was Hama; then fifty-eight to Ma'arat before the final eighty kilometres to Aleppo. Once through that city it was only half-an-hour to the border . . .

They reached Ma'arat at 3.35. Twenty kilometres further on, just as they were feeling confident, and were admiring the peak of Jel Sawiya gliding past them to the westward, Kim stiffened by his side. 'Don't look round, Dirk,' she said, not loud enough for their passengers to hear. 'There was a police jeep down that track off to the left.'

Dirk felt the kick in his stomach. He would know shortly whether the Syrians would try to arrest them. He stabbed at the accelerator. The game little Peugeot roared its response and he forced her on with all the power he could extract. Then the idea came to him, suddenly – but he needed a moment to think it through. . . . Supposing their two passengers weren't friendly? They weren't saying much. . . .

The car was surging along now, enjoying the test: 140 kmh – and not labouring too badly. If he could hold this for an hour and a bit, he would feel better. Then, as they dropped again into the plain, he heard the words he was dreading . . .

'They're after us,' Kim said quietly. 'Several kilometres behind, I'd say. They don't seem to be gaining.'

'Get my registration book out of my wallet,' he snapped. 'The insurance certificate is in the locker.' He handed her his wallet. He talked quickly over his shoulder: 'We don't know who you are, but we're leaving you at the next turn. Hand us the food haversack and my grip, will you?'

He heard them muttering to themselves.

'It's okay. You can have the car and do what you like with it. Give 'em the documents, Kim, and scribble out an authority saying that we've loaned them the car.'

10

'We'll go through Aleppo,' said the man in the back, 'then to the Turkish border. What'll we do with the car when we're through with it?' The student's breath was hot on Dirk's neck, and the American accent grated – the product of the local university, no doubt.

'Get rid of it. Destroy it somehow. It's all yours, chum. Here's the turn . . . we're baling out. All set, Kim?'

He heard her nervous assent and when the signpost, 12 *Idlib*, came up, he stopped the car. He left it running, jumped out and shoved the man into the driving seat. He grabbed the haversack beneath the student's feet.

'Got everything, Kim?'

'Yes, Mr Trevallack.'

He ran round the back of the brake and rapped on the roof. 'Good luck. Drive like hell.'

The engine raced abominably, there was a splutter of gravel at the rear tyres and the two youngsters were off, bemused by their sudden luck.

'Quick. Off the road.'

He pushed her onwards towards the pitted rocks skirting the road. 'Get a move on, Kim. If we're spotted now, we might as well turn up our toes.' His ears strained for the sound of approaching traffic and then he heard it, a police siren, blaring its disconcerting warning from somewhere behind them. He pulled the woman down to the ground and curled up beside her on the far side of a group of boulders where a line of scrub ran the length of the hollow. Cautiously he raised his head, keeping his hand on her shoulder, forcing her to lie still. He could see the four policemen, straining forwards in their seats as they roared by in their military jeep. He watched the truck disappearing into the distance, then allowed Kim Quintan to sit up.

'Over the road, quick.'

They scrambled back to the tarmac, then ran the fifty metres to the Idlib turn which led off to their left. If they could put the shoulder of the hill between them and the main road, before any further traffic approached, they would be safe.

'Give me the food sack. We'll lie up for a spell and work things out.' He took Kim's hand and led her back into the scrub, whence they could watch the Idlib road. He threw himself down and arranged the haversacks as a back-rest for her.

'I'm afraid I'm holding you up,' she said smiling wanly, as wearily she slumped to the ground. 'Something to eat?' She held out a packet of boiled sweets and a hunk of goat's cheese.

'Thanks. I'm so hungry, I can even eat that.' He smiled as she held out a bottle of Coca-Cola. 'And even drink that', and he winced as the sickly stuff ran down his gullet. Thirst was bothering him more than hunger. 'Got the map?'

They relaxed for the first time since this long day had begun. Spreading out the map on the brown soil, their escape plan was beginning to take shape. It was twelve kilometres to Idlib which, by the look of it, was a sizeable town compared to the village of Bennich which lay only a few kilometres ahead.

'It's 4.25,' Kim said. 'Too late to phone Ankara now. It's dark by 5.30.'

'England is on GMT and is an hour behind us. If we can get through, why don't we try head office before they pack up for the day? The Foreign Department will be expecting something from us and may even be keeping an all-night service going.

'Come on then . . . what are you waiting for, Mr Trevallack?'

She jumped up and was even holding out a hand to haul him to his feet. Dirk smiled at her: at last, she was unbending. They re-joined the road and started walking steadily westwards towards the town of Idlib. They sought cover when two cars passed them, one in either direction. They were about to dive again, when Dirk recognized the unmistakable sound of a diesel. He held Kim's wrist and waited.

A yellow bus, with rusty red trimmings, bucketed round the turn. Dirk waved it down and pushed Kim up into the foul-smelling interior. The vehicle was packed with school children and one of them had obviously been sick. Dirk held out a handful of Syrian coins towards the driver who took the fares dispassionately. The chatter died for a moment, while the two foreigners were regarded by the young Syrians. A couple of kids jumped up and offered their seats to the silent strangers. Dirk thankfully accepted and then the noise began as rapidly as it had subsided. The bus worked up to its maximum speed and began careering down the road.

'Bit of luck,' Dirk muttered. 'Hope the thing goes to Idlib. Could you read the board on the front?'

'We're okay. Idlib and Chorhour.' The bus-load of children soon forgot their inarticulate passengers. Dirk was beginning to feel the tension passing from him, when he caught the driver's eye peering at him from the mirror. Dirk met his eye but the man swiftly resumed his concentration.

The evening was already drawing in when the bus finally drew up at the main square in Idlib, having jettisoned half its load in the village of Bennich. Nonchalantly following the last child out of the bus, Dirk nodded to the driver, then helped Kim down with the haversacks. As they strolled away from the stop, the driver was talking confidentially to a grubby, uniformed official – an inspector by the look of him.

'Out of the square,' Dirk whispered. 'We're too conspicuous here. Play the part of British tourists, if we're interrogated. Take my arm.'

Together they strolled around the open square of the fly-blown town of Idlib. The smell of the drains permeated every street and there was garbage lying in the gutters where the dogs had been scavenging. On the far side of the market place stood one hotel. Lights were already shining from its windows.

'We'll ask for rooms in the café. Come on. You'll have to drink with me.' He chuckled and, to his surprise, she did not relinquish his arm. He bundled her through the door of the Elysée Café, a squalid bar reeking of spirits and which wore the unmistakable French style of yesteryear. The Syrians had remained good friends with the French since the colonial days.

'Two Pernods.' He spoke in his best French. The pallid barman flipped the drinks across the dirty bartop. Dirk watched the liquid clouding when the water was added.

'Where can we sleep for the night?'

'Hotel?'

'An *auberge* will do us.' The Arab grinned, laid his finger to his nose and pointed down the narrow street leading off to the left. Dirk looked away for, with her colouring, Kim blushed easily.

'First turn left,' the man said. 'Pension Nasser.'

Dirk knocked back the drink, picked up the gear and led the way out. They turned down the darkened lane where, at the end, a dimly lit, depressing building stood in the shadows.

'Don't like the look of it,' Dirk said, 'but we'll be safe here.' He sensed Kim's reluctance, but she remained silent. He pushed open the ramshackle door, waited for her to join him in the gloomy hall then rang the handbell on the reception desk. There was a stirring from behind the grubby red curtains and an unwashed crone with straggly hair shuffled towards them.

'You do the talking, Kim.'

They were led up a flight of creaking wooden steps to a room on the first floor. The old woman opened a door, then switched on the dim light dangling from the ceiling. The room was minute. There was barely enough room to negotiate the double bed. Kim twitched at the purple bedspread, saw the grubby sheets. She glanced over her shoulder at Dirk.

'We'll take it,' he said.

The crone mumbled and handed the key to Kim.

'There's a loo down the passage and a communal wash-place,' Kim said. 'And she'll knock us up a cous-cous.'

'I'm ravenous,' he said, when the door had closed on them. 'Let's get organized quickly and then eat.'

They spread the map on the bed. It was a hundred kilometres to Latakia, over the hills and across the Orontes river to the plain. 'She told me the bus ran every three hours,' Kim said. 'Two hours to Latakia, via Chorhour. Apparently the route runs round the Ansariya escarpment, then down the Kebir river valley to the sea.'

'We'll phone from here in the morning, if we can. Safer than in Latakia. I reckon we ought to get through to head office. We're so near the Turkish border, we could hike over it and reach Iskenderon: there's a railway direct to Ankara from there. The sooner we hand over this lot to the consul, the happier I'll be. Let's eat.'

'Wouldn't it be safer to split the money?' Kim asked. 'I don't feel safe here, do you?'

They divided the cash between them. Dirk tied the notes around his stomach, inside a sock from the pair he had slung into his grip. Kim took the bonds, cards and traveller's cheques. She tucked the bonds and cheques into the bottom of her sling bag and, turning her back, slipped the cards into her bra.

'Excuse me,' she said. 'I'll be back in a moment.'

Dirk waited, hands in his pockets, looking out of the window. The moon hung behind the houses and the shadows ran long and dark across the walls and roofs. He was not used to living at close quarters with a woman. Mrs Quintan had little sense of humour, as far as he could tell. This was going to be a difficult night, but at least he had thrown their pursuers off the track – and he smiled to himself. He was glad he had saved the cash and the codes from those ruthless bastards who were shooting it out in the bank.

The door opened and she stood there, neat as ever, in her open-necked shirt, traditional Shetland jersey and practical jeans. Shyly she held out her hand to him. 'I'm ready to dine with you, Mr Trevallack,' she mocked. 'Will you accompany me to the dining-room?'

He followed her out, the code haversack dangling from his wrist. At least, in her cosy way, she was beginning to thaw. He might even like her by the time they reached Ankara. But how the hell was he going to cope with her tonight? It was still only just seven, and they would have to doss down early . . .

The meal was ample and surprisingly good. A carafe of rough, red wine soothed his nerves and by the time they had paid for the room and meal, the future was looking distinctly rosier. He had deliberately not forced the vino on Kim.

'I drink very little,' she said as she sipped at the warming wine. 'And I want to sleep tonight.' For an instant, her eye caught his and she looked away, blushing again.

'We'll turn in early,' he said. 'You never know what tomorrow will bring.' They strolled out into the little garden. The lattice-work of moonshine criss-crossed the rectangle of coarse grass and from somewhere he heard the chanting of Arabian singing. A cat was miaowing from the spread-eagled fig tree, leafless now, that sprawled against the wall beneath the window of their shuttered room.

'Come on, Mrs Quintan,' he said roughly. 'Bed. We'll be up early in the morning.'

She said nothing, but led the way back into the inn. The stairs subsided beneath the weight of their bodies and the floorboards creaked as they tip-toed down the corridor.

'Have you got your spanner?' she whispered.

He nodded and opened the door. She did not switch on the light, but slipped to the near side of the bed. Dirk left her for a moment and after returning from the odiferous lavatory, he closed the door of their bedroom and turned the lock on the inside, leaving the key in the lock. He tip-toed to the far side of the bed and opened the shutters and windows.

'Not too cold?' he asked. 'I like the air on my face.'

'Me too,' she murmured. He remained standing, staring through the prussian blue rectangle. 'Get undressed,' he said over his shoulder. 'I'm sleeping on the floor.'

15

He heard the rustle of her clothes, then the creaking of the bed. He turned and opened the plywood wardrobe. He tossed her a pillow, keeping the other and the blanket for himself.

'Okay?' he asked. 'Not too cold?'

He heard her contented sigh as she pulled the bedclothes about her. In the faint light from the moon, he could distinguish the outline of her head on the pillow.

'I'll sing out if I'm cold,' she whispered. 'Goodnight, Dirk.'

He slipped out of his shirt and trousers, rolled into the double blanket doubling it around himself like a cocoon.

' 'Night, Kim. Thanks for today.'

There was no reply and all he could hear was her regular breathing. At least, she did not snore. . . . It had all been easier than he had imagined. Bloody stupid, what mountains people made out of convention. Cleaning your teeth, washing, dressing, bodily functions – modesty vanished and the veneer of modern inhibitions soon evaporated under duress. He drowsed off into sleep. . . . Kim Quintan was not the prude he had judged her to be.

Chapter 3

It was already mid-afternoon when Dirk and Kim reached Latakia harbour and its cluster of shipping offices along the waterfront. The couple were tired and hungry after their long slog yesterday.

Dirk sensed that they had been traced to Idlib. Through the window of the filthy lavatory in the inn, he had sighted two Syrian police talking with the old woman on the steps outside the entrance. And when, at three in the morning, Kim had been awoken by the sound of someone trying the lock of their door, he had decided to bale out.

The moon had set when they scrambled down that fig-tree outside their window. They had escaped unnoticed through the garden and had cleared Idlib without incident. He had decided to keep off the main roads, so they walked due westward along a dust track that crossed the plain. Their last meal today, Friday, had been at 7.30 this morning in Quafar, a country town near the left bank of the Orontes river.

It had taken five hours to contact the bank in London. The line from the only telephone in the market town had been abominable, but Henderson, the Director of the BB's Foreign Division, had been pleased to have been put in the picture. By using question and answer (Dick was sure that the line was being monitored), Henderson had shot down Dirk's proposal to cross over the border and to reach Iskenderon in Turkey. From there, Ankara would have been easy, but the consul had warned that all roads, trains and airports were being watched.

'OEDIPUS expected at Istanbul,' Henderson had concluded. 'We'll leave it to you. I'll explain when you next call . . . OEDIPUS Istanbul – understood understood?' – and he had rung off.

Finally, after an excruciating trip in a school-bus, they had reached this fly-blown port of Latakia. At last they felt that the heat of the chase had lessened, but their morale had slumped, when, after all their efforts, they learned that the next ship that would accept passengers for Istanbul was not sailing until next Wednesday, 30 December.

'While you were arguing with the shipping clerk, I did some shopping,' Kim said, as she shyly pressed a small parcel into his hand. 'Happy Christmas.'

He looked down at her. She was trying to smile, but the tears were near.

He stared across the ancient harbour – and this was once the Holy Land. . . . The gulls were flapping lazily down the coast and a heat haze hung, dancing its mirages upon the horizon and the somnolent port. Kim and he had come a long way – but they were embroiled up to the neck in something not of their making. If they stayed here until Wednesday, they could be run to earth. The Syrians were on a war footing these days.

'And to you too, Kim.' He bent down and pecked her cheek. 'Happy Christmas. Let's celebrate it with a decent lunch.'

The café overlooked the inner harbour where the fishing boats were moored. As they sat drinking their rosé and enjoying their fish, Dirk idly regarded the old caique lying stern on to the quay. Her grey sides were red-splotched where the galvanized fastenings were rusting through; her dirty sails lay untidily bundled along her booms; she was trimmed to the waterline and ready for sea. A bearded giant was working on his charts in the wheelhouse, while a dark-skinned, moustachioed seaman sprawled along the transom, eyeing the populace passing by. He hailed a fisherman who was *en route* to his boat, but the man shook his head, spat into the water and continued on his way. Then Dirk noticed the painted sign propped against the gangway. 'What's that read?' he asked Kim. 'You're the Arabic expert.'

'I was just trying to unravel it,' she said laughing, 'but now that I've got it, I'm not telling you . . .'

'Come on . . .' Her coyness was irritating him but the contentment of the post-lunch and wine was having its effect. Drowsiness was dulling his senses and he felt that the world, though infantile in its politics, was good. 'Let's have it, Kim – so long as it's not indecent . . .'

'*Mate and deckhand wanted,*' she read, not heeding him. 'I can't make out the rest, but it's something to do with the captain . . .'

He sat there staring at the old ship – probably nearly fifty years old, but fitted now with diesels, as were all these coasters. She had probably transported German troops through the Greek islands during Hitler's war.

'Well, Kim, are you game? It's one way of getting out, so long as she's bound for Greece, Turkey or anywhere westwards.'

'I used to sail a bit with my father . . . know a few knots.'

'That'll do . . . and with the knife you've just given me, *Kaso* couldn't wish for better hands.' The caique's name, in peeling green paint, was painted in bold letters, but her port of registry, Salonika, was almost illegible.

'Let's try, Kim.' She nodded her assent. 'Stay here, then; order the coffee while I talk to her skipper.'

Floyd Lievenow reached for his spectacles. Thirty-seven next month, he was beginning to need them for distinguishing the sounding lines on these charts of the Aegean. He had been skipper of this old caique for nearly nine months and was enjoying the job. The excitement of coast-crawling and sailing most of the time compensated in large measure for the excitement of the inshore work he had been carrying out as a young USN lieutenant through the mess of Vietnam. He had been unable to settle to the disloyalties and boredom of civilian life. When 'doing' Greece, he had run across Ed Hansen in Piraeus. Floyd had thankfully accepted the offer of running one of Ed's caiques which comprised part of the Hansen Coastal Company. Floyd's naval certificates had circumvented the requirements of bureaucracy, but Ed had always been up to something, skating the edge of the law, even in the States. Floyd asked no questions and took the job. He had not been the least surprised when, on his second trip to Salonika, he had discovered the dope amongst his innocent cargo of cotton and carpets. He obeyed without questioning and took the stuff where he was ordered. *Kaso*'s modern radio equipment kept him in touch with Hansen who ran his office from Istanbul – this roving existence stimulated Lievenow and he enjoyed drifting with life's tide.

He pricked off the distance to the Otranto straits – 740 kilometres. As soon as he could make up his crew, he would slip and be under way for Istanbul, his port of arrival according to Ed's latest instructions. The cargo was stowed and *Kaso* had cleared customs.

'Someone to see you, Skip,' Paulos croaked through the wheelhouse door. 'Says he's English.'

' 'kay. Bring the guy aboard.'

The man who elbowed his way through the wheelhouse door could be no other than a limey. He was powerfully built, of about

Floyd's height, and could be useful in a hassle. About twenty-eight probably and had been around a bit. His heavy shoes were covered in dust and he looked weary. He wore thick-lensed, rimless glasses.

Floyd questioned the Brit closely, but Trevallack was not giving much away. Been a marine, he said, knew how to steer and keep a watch. Eyesight was no problem and his companion, though a woman, understood the sea. Floyd hestiated.

On principle, he was anti-limey. His father, who had been a captain USN, was a rabid mid-westerner and psychopathic towards the British. Lievenow Snr. had been quietly removed from his post during World War II for his ridiculous attitude when dealing with limeys – and a little of this contagion had rubbed off on his son, Floyd acknowledged to himself.

'Yeah ... I'll take you, but, for formality's sake, I'll have to charge you a dollar each to sign you on.' He grinned and inclined his head towards the café where Trevallack's bird was patiently waiting. 'Keep an eye on her, Trevallack. My crew aren't a fussy lot.'

The Brit nodded, the brown eyes steady behind those spectacles. 'What time do you want us on board?' he asked, ignoring the warning.

'I'm sailing at dusk. Six o'clock will do.'

'Thanks. We'll be here.'

The Brit completed the register and handed over a couple of dollars. 'Your girl can sign later,' Floyd said. 'Paulos will show you your bunks. You can have No. 5, the only one with any privacy. Your gear will be safe aboard. Heh – Paulos.'

The Greek shambled across the gangway, his eyes everywhere.

'Thanks,' said Trevallack. 'I'll get Kim's stuff.'

Floyd watched the couple reorganizing their gear in the café. They seemed to take an inordinate amount of time, but eventually the limey returned to dump his gear, having left a couple of bags with the girl.

Floyd watched them strolling off along the waterfront. They seemed harmless enough, but life had hardened Floyd who now trusted no one. When he saw them entering the 'poste', he began to wonder; they were too old for student bravado, and tourists, even when broke, preferred to travel more comfortably than by caique. They were running from something, he was sure of it.

The Englishman was an unusual one: not as snotty as most, but there was something about him that was out of the ordinary.

Though he looked over-weight, the bitter lines at the corner of his mouth and the compressed lips suggested a self-discipline alien to these indulgent days.

Floyd reached for the almanac above him. He had better hurry, or his passage plan would not be ready by sailing time – and from past experience, he knew he could not cope without this essential pre-planning. He might be casual in his personal life, but in his navigation, never; he was the only competent seafarer aboard this caique. He was not going to be caught out twice. The memory of the night when a block had pole-axed him remained a nightmare. On the lee shore off Leros, there was no one else in *Kaso* who could lay a course and the caique was within a cable of foundering on the rocks. If Trevallack had not turned up he would not be sailing tonight without Philos, his trained radio-hand who had gone sick. Trevallack had experienced radio work whilst in the marines and had been watch-keeping in the British Navy – and Floyd began laying off his course for the Skarpanto Strait and on to Istanbul: ETA midday Tuesday, the twenty-ninth, all things being equal. After dumping the stuff (Turkey was the middle-east transit point for dope, it seemed) *Kaso* was to load with tobacco. She was to return to Piraeus where Hansen would issue fresh orders for the month of February. Floyd sighed. One more trip and he was having his over-due vacation . . .

They joined *Kaso* at 5.30, having had enough time comfortably to stroll around the town after phoning London from the harbour post office. Dirk had been put through remarkably smoothly and it had been good to have longer with Henderson who certainly ran the Foreign Department efficiently. By again using question and answer they had carried on a lucid conversation. Dirk had given Monday or Tuesday as their arrival at Istanbul, and Henderson would arrange for the Consul to be ready, night or day, to receive OEDIPUS. Though Henderson had sounded pleased enough, he had re-emphasized that extreme caution was needed. Apparently, Dirk's successful escape with the bank's assets had infuriated the middle-eastern authorities who were determined to prevent him leaving the area. So aircraft, railways, and particularly the roads, were dangerous – and Henderson sounded relieved by Dirk's news. The Director seemed surprised that Mrs Quintan was with him, but had understood the need for an adequate interpreter.

'We'll feed on board,' Dirk told Kim. 'Wouldn't do any harm to get to know the hands before we sail.'

They were shown to their quarters by Paulos. Kim had behaved calmly and displayed no surprise when shown to her bunk. Descending the central ladder, their bunks, one above the other, were on the port side, for'd, abreast the step of the mast. A table stood in the centre of the messdeck, the bunks lining the ship's side. The berths were screened by grubby curtains. Dirk heaved Kim's gear on to the upper bunk and then they unpacked what was necessary on Dirk's berth below. What to do with the codes and the securities was the urgent problem.

There was a locker for each of the five crew: Paulos, the bo'sun; Philos, the absent radio-hand; and the two Greek seamen, Souphlos and Arto who seemed friendly enough when the two foreigners joined them on their messdeck. Arto was the more formidable of the two, a heavy, blue-jowled man of about forty, with sly, sunken eyes. Souphlos was half asleep and smelt of drink. Both sported long knives in leather scabbards.

Paulos could speak enough English to make himself understood. His two gold teeth gleamed from the light of the oil lamps which had already been lit. He spread wide his hands: 'We eat now,' he grinned. 'No Eeenglish food, unless Miss would like cooking.'

From this moment Kim became the ship's cook. She accepted the role stoically and her willingness immediately began demolishing the barriers. By eight o'clock, when the hands were called by the captain, even Souphlos was laughing. 'The girl can stay below to clean up,' the skipper shouted. 'Paulos, you work the ship. Trevallack come into the wheelhouse with me.'

Dirk heard the whirring of the starters and then the sudden shuddering of the caique's hull as her two diesels pulsed into life.

'Let go aft. Heave in for'd.'

Floyd Lievenow leaned out of the wheelhouse window to watch the cable being hove in. *Kaso* slid slowly ahead, the boats on either side of her scraping along her scarred sides. Then she was clear and, as she manœuvred towards the breakwater, Dirk watched Souphlos and Arto stowing the oil-smeared fenders. The hands were singing softly to themselves as they secured the ship for sea.

'They're glad to be out of this dump,' Floyd said. 'There's nothing for them here. They'll get their run ashore in Istanbul;

won't see Arto for days. He always jumps ship there – he's tangled with a Turkish lady who never lets him go.'

The skipper was talking to himself and Dirk remained silent, too preoccupied with his thoughts to heed the monologue. If Kim could remain cook for the trip, she would be able to keep an eye on the codes if he stowed them in the lockers. So far everyone seemed friendly enough. He leaned out of the opposite window as the caique slowly headed for the harbour entrance. It was dark now and the lights of the coasters and fishing boats were gleaming across the surface of the black water.

'It's a fine sight by daylight, Trevallack,' Lievenow said. 'The rocks on the shore line gleam white and when there's shade they're all colours of the rainbow, from pale green to deep violet. You can just see Jebel Aqra, all by itself to the northward' – and he pointed across the harbour to the distant loom of the lonely mountain, its peak piercing the night clouds which were sailing in from the west.

Dirk was watching the coastline sliding past, when he sighted the side lights of a launch moving at speed across the harbour, a bow wave at her forefoot. Lievenow was cursing quietly to himself.

'That's the police boat,' he said. 'What the hell's she after at this time of night? They usually leave the sailings to the customs' launch and I've cleared with them.' He stretched across and eased the revs, as the launch spluttered alongside, five metres off their starboard quarter.

'*Kaso*,' Lievenow bellowed above the plopping of the caique's cooling outlets. 'Bound for Istanbul.'

A Syrian voice shouted back from the dimly lit cockpit of the launch. The broken English was intelligible enough in the darkness.

'Okay, Floyd,' the voice crackled through the loud-hailer. 'Sulim here. The customs are searching the harbour for a couple of English on the run. They might have reached Latakia, so we're making sure. You know what the Chief's like . . .' and the Syrian laughed in the darkness. 'D'you make up your crew all right?'

Dirk slowly nodded his head and shrugged his shoulders, as he met the skipper's glance. For a long moment the two men stared at each other in the gloom of the wheelhouse. 'Give us a break,' Dirk murmured. 'We're not criminals – just trying to get out.' He held his breath while Lievenow hesitated. If the American handed him over, *Kaso* would have to return to harbour. He could not work the ship with two hands short . . .

'Floyd, you okay?' Sulim persisted. 'Is your register complete?'

'Yeah, thanks.' Nonchalantly he slid back the door of the wheel-house, then moved out on to the deck. 'Couple of layabouts. They'll have to do, I guess, until Istanbul. See you next month, Sulim. Thanks for the wine this morning. . . . See you,' and he returned to the throttle controls. The diesels chugged up to cruising revs and Dirk felt the caique surging towards the open sea. The swell hit them and the police boat swirled round in a smother of foam, as she thrashed back to harbour.

Floyd Lievenow slammed the door and took the wheel. Darkness descended and then *Kaso* was plunging into the swell. He stuck his head through the window and yelled for'd: 'Hoist all plain sail. Set night watches, Paulos.' He turned to Dirk who stood motionless in the corner of the dimly lit wheelhouse. 'Give 'em a hand for'd, Trevallack. Arto's got the middle and Souphlos works with him – starboard watch. Paulos and you are port watch and have the first, eight till midnight.'

'Thanks,' Dirk said. He moved towards the door.

'When you come back,' Lievenow said quietly, 'you've some explaining to do, Trevallack.'

Chapter 4

The plodding of the diesels, and the creaking of the mainsheet and peak halyard blocks were having a disastrous effect on Dirk's ability to keep awake. This period of the morning watch, between seven and eight on a winter's morning, was always the most difficult in which to remain alert. His eyes ached with trying to prevent his lids from closing.

'You make up log, Dirk?' Paulos called from the wheel. 'You do that?'

The smell of coffee was percolating up from the messdeck where he could see the bottom of Kim's jeans moving briskly across the deck as she threw the breakfast together. A south-easterly breeze had sprung up with the dawn and *Kaso*, which was a good seaboat, was rolling along merrily in this quarter sea. Kim's bunk was just visible from the corner of the wheelhouse door, so Dirk could keep an eye on her when he was on watch. So far so good. She had been left alone – even an Arab can recognize a cold 'un when he saw one – and Dirk had been at pains last night to mention that he was a trained killer if need be. Since then, Arto and Souphlos had kept well clear. They made themselves understood only when they needed help on deck.

Breakfast would prove what sort of trip this was to be. . . . There was an atmosphere of hostility on the messdeck when the watches had changed, but this may have been jealousy because of Dirk's privileged position with the skipper; or, the crew's resentment when Dirk had locked his locker every time he went to it. Though theft was no sin in their eyes, no one liked being called a thief. There was no other stowage for the haversack containing the codes. And, if Arto and his mate were light-fingered, they had been foiled so far. With either Kim or both of them always on the messdeck, and Dirk so close at hand, there should be no trouble . . .

Kaso left Cape Andreas abeam at five o'clock. As Dirk completed the eight o'clock log, he could see the faint line of blue hills of Cyprus cutting above the southern horizon. Dawn was breaking astern of them, the clouds pink with the new day. '08.00, Saturday,

26 December,' Dirk wrote in the log. 'Wind ENE, force five,' and the barometer was falling. 'Course 275, Speed 10·7 knots.' *Kaso* was heeling now and was picking up her skirts. If this wind held, they could make their ETA, Istanbul – Tuesday, forenoon. He opened the leeward window and gulped a deep breath of this soft air. Paulos's foul Turkish cigarette smoke had been choking the wheel-house for the past four hours and there had been moments when Dirk had felt the first qualms of nausea.

A school of dolphins was cruising along joyously off their port bow, their gleaming bodies prancing in attendance with the caique.

'Sign of good luck,' the skipper said as he approached Dirk quietly through the door. 'Where are we?'

Dirk indicated their 08.00 position. 'Couldn't get a fix. This is our DR –' and he pointed to the pencilled circle forty-six kilometres northward of the long finger that was the coastline of Cyprus. Lievenow studied the chart in silence. He had not again referred to their conversation of last night, when he had listened to Dirk's brief account of their escape from the Lebanon. So far, Dirk had succeeded in concealing the reason for their sudden exit. Lebanon was no place to be in at this moment and this had satisfied Lievenow, it seemed.

Arto and Souphlos moved silently through the door. Paulos handed over the watch and Dirk went below.

'Breakfast's ready,' Kim said. She gave a bleak smile as Paulos squeezed his way past her. 'English breakfast, no?' he grinned.

The coffee and the black bread went down well and by the time they had moved again to the upper deck Paulos was becoming talkative.

'Leave the crocks to me,' Kim said as she cleared away. 'I'm enjoying myself in the galley.' They piled the stuff into the sink and left her to it. They went on deck and all that morning they scrubbed and washed down. They ate at noon (Kim had provided vegetable soup and fried chicken, even though the caique was moving about). By four o'clock, half-a-gale was blowing and *Kaso* was clocking up eight knots, even without the diesels which the skipper had stopped. The caique crossed the Gulf of Antalya during the night and on Sunday morning at dawn, the skipper was surprised to sight Kastelrozzo on their starboard beam – about twenty-four kilometres off.

'She always does this,' Lievenow said. 'With a quartering sea, she yaws up to windward, however hard we try to hold her. He crouched over the chart and rammed himself into the corner to prevent himself being hurled about. 'Bring her round to 265°, Trevallack.'

'Steady on 265°. . . .' Dirk was enjoying himself. Wrestling with the wheel was exhilarating after so long ashore. Kim had ventured on deck for only a few brief spells. Even with *Kaso*'s corkscrewing, the girl seemed unaffected by sea-sickness, but Dirk was happier up top. The smell of food and the slosh of bilge water beneath their feet had made him sick during the night. If things became any worse he would be disgracing himself again. He stayed on the upper deck for as long as he could and skipped the midday meal.

By Sunday afternoon, *Kaso* was rolling on her beam ends, but she remained reasonably dry. Paulos and the hands were splicing the new warps, so Dirk had a chance to slip below. He left the sound of Paulos's singing behind him and floundered into the messdeck. Kim was stretched out in her bunk. He collapsed on to the mess stool below her.

'How d'you manage it?' he groaned as the nausea swept over him. 'The smell's enough for me.' The stench from the greasy oil-cloth covering the table was another insidious odour infecting the atmosphere.

Kim slid quietly from her bunk. She led him across to the star-board side where they were invisible from the wheelhouse. She bent down and began prising one of the deck boards.

'What are you up to?' Dirk asked her as he took over. 'Is the ship making water?'

The boards came up. Below their feet swilled the filthy bilge water, its surface a film of oily scum. By the dim light percolating from above, he glimpsed row upon row of shining tins, each stowed neatly between the frames.

'The board broke adrift during one of our heavy rolls,' Kim whispered. 'I re-stowed them but snitched a tin to see if I could use it in the galley. Hurry, shut it up again.'

Her secrecy irritated him. All he wanted was to reach the upper before he puked.

'Quick, Dirk. What d'you make of this?'

She led him back to her bunk. From beneath the blanket she extracted another of the tins. The lid was opened and when she had regained the privacy of the seaboard side, she held the tin to his nose. The smell was strangely familiar and the contents were unappetisingly brown. There were serial numbers on the outside of the tin. He had been put through the drug course in the Royals, and opium had always been easy to identify.

'What d'you think it is?' he retaliated.

'Hashish or some sort of drug.'

'Opium. Sure of it . . . and there were hundreds of tins stowed away down there.' Keeping his back to the companionway, he opened his locker and pushed the tin inside. 'No time to talk now,' he said. 'We'll have to think this out. They'll smell the stuff if we don't get rid of it.'

'Leave me your key,' she said. 'I'll ditch the tin with the rubbish. Stay in the wheelhouse and I'll pass the bucket up to you. Empty it over the stern and no one will notice. I'll call when I'm ready.' She was all bustle and efficiency.

He rushed up the ladder and cleared the wheelhouse as the sickness overwhelmed him. Leaning over the port quarter, he retched out his insides. Then he heard the skipper calling.

'Take her, Trevallack. I'm taking a running fix on Kastelrozzo.'

The caique took some holding. Yawing up to windward, it was exhausting work to prevent her broaching-to. Lievenow was stepping back into the wheelhouse, hand-bearing compass in his hand, when a woman's voice called up from below: 'Dirk, throw this overboard for me, will you?'

Taking his eyes from the whirling compass for a second, he saw her there, red hair pushed back, the overloaded bucket perched precariously upon the top step.

'Give it here.' Lievenow was reaching down and without further ado, he grabbed at the handle and yanked the bucket through the leeward door. He stumbled outside and from the corner of his eye, Dirk saw him emptying the rubbish over the side. Finally, to make sure there were no scraps left, he banged the rim hard upon the gunwale. The gulls screamed around the floating rubbish, as the tins and scraps bobbed along in the wash before disappearing in the foaming seas astern.

Kim's face had disappeared from the ladder. Lievenow was strolling to the port quarter. He remained there for some time before returning slowly to the messdeck ladder. 'Here's your bucket,' he called. 'There was certainly a lot of garbage, cookie.'

Dirk kept his eye on the compass needle, as he felt the skipper's eyes upon him. The buffeting of the wind upon the wheelhouse, the snatches of song from the hands for'd and the gurgling of the seas in the leeward scuppers were the only sounds. Lievenow studied the chart again, turned his back and went below to his cabin.

Alone for the rest of the forenoon, Dirk tried to work out his future course of action. Even if Lievenow had rumbled that they had found the dope, there was nothing to be gained at this instant for Dirk to disclose the fact of their discovery. Neither side was positive of the other. Dirk would keep quiet, but he and Kim would snatch their sleep during alternate watches from now on – and he felt the comforting weight of his seaman's knife which he had spliced to a lanyard . . .

The rest of Sunday passed without incident. The skipper got his head down during the afternoon and surfaced only when the island of Rhodes was sighted at dusk. At nine o'clock he rounded up and laid his course for the Skarpanto Strait. He wore the caique round, and then she became unmanageable. Just as Lievenow had decided to tack down wind, the gale seemed to ease: by the beginning of the eight-to-twelve, the guts had gone out of it.

Dirk was thankful to find his berth. Kim was waiting in her bunk above him, prepared to remain awake until four, when Dirk would be going on watch again for the morning. Paulos's snores grunted from the dimness of the opposite side of the messdeck. 'Dirk,' she whispered from behind her curtain. 'Did he see it?'

'Reckon so. He hasn't said a word.'

'What'll he do?'

'They can rush us any time they like. Our best chance is to know nothing. None of our business – we should be in Istanbul tomorrow. Keep going as you are. You're doing fine, girl.'

He climbed into his bunk and tucked the knife by his side. He left the curtain undrawn. He lost consciousness as his head hit the straw-filled pillow.

First, he felt the pressure on his shoulder. Then he heard her voice whispering above him as she leaned down to wake him. He was awake and saw the cleavage of her breasts in her open-necked shirt. With a shock, he realized for the first time that Mrs Quintan was not so unattractive after all. Perhaps it was the closeness of her out here in the open seas, or perhaps she was losing her aloofness . . . and then he heard the crackling of the radio from the wheelhouse.

Lievenow was talking on the R/T, his words indistinguishable amidst the clutter of the caique's sea-music.

Dirk had remained fully dressed, so he slipped from his bunk and scrambled up the ladder. Arto was on the wheel, Souphlos was asleep on his haunches in the corner and the skipper was bent over the radio mouthpiece, trying to conceal his conversation. Dirk stood beside him, ready to take the message.

'Okay, Ed. Got your message. See you. *OUT.*'

Lievenow snapped the phone back into its rack. He turned and faced Dirk, before reaching for his parallel ruler.

'That was the boss,' he said coldly. 'We're to deliver the goods to Trieste.' He snipped off the distances with his dividers, across the Sea of Crete, up the Ionian Sea and into the Adriatic. He stabbed a point into the Gulf of Venice. 'Trieste,' he said. 'Between eight and midnight, next Friday, New Year's day. Suits us fine.'

'Why?' Dirk asked, his patience running out. 'It's a disaster for us. We're expected in Istanbul tomorrow.'

'Too bad, Trevallack. I obey orders. What's your hurry, anyway?'

Dirk could see the hostility in the American's eyes. Behind him he heard the rustle of Souphlos climbing to his feet. Dirk backed to the opened lee door. Here, he could block the gangway to the messdeck and Kim.

'No chance of an earlier port of arrival?' Dirk asked. 'Piraeus . . . Salonika?'

Floyd Lievenow laughed harshly. 'You're paid also to obey orders. Goddammit, man, who the hell d'you think you are?' He beat his fist on the chart table. 'You're on the run. I've asked no questions, but what d'you mean by snooping about my ship?' He was advancing towards Dirk, his eyes blazing. 'What guarantee have I that you won't shop us to Interpol the moment we hit port?' He opened his mouth and bellowed towards the hatch for Paulos.

'Okay, limey. You've asked for it – what are you going to do about it?'

The world was crashing about Dirk's ears. He was powerless if they rushed him now. A couple of bodies over the side and into the Sea of Crete – lost at sea and no one the wiser. He heard Paulos behind him clattering up the ladder, felt the knife in his back. The blade pricked as *Kaso* wallowed at her new course.

'I couldn't care less about the dope you're carrying,' Dirk shouted. 'If you kill us, you'll be hunted until you're found. *Our* boss knows that we are taking passage with you. When we don't turn up in Istanbul, he'll set Interpol after you. You can dump the dope if you like, but they'll get you for murder. All we ask is to be put ashore at the nearest European port.'

'D'you mean that? You'll keep your trap shut?' Lievenow was looking towards the hatchway and his command rapped again. 'Try anything, woman, and we'll slit your throat . . .'

Dirk heard Kim's cry as Paulos slammed her in the stomach. He heard her tumbling down the ladder.

'Okay, Trevallack. We need your help on this trip. You play ball and we'll put you ashore in Trieste. You can phone Istanbul on the R/T if you like. We'll be out of range by morning.'

'Will you allow me to put a message through for delivery to the Consul?'

'Yeah, but don't try anything. I'll be right behind you.'

The pressure of the knife eased. Lievenow was already getting through to Istanbul radio. By 2.30 the message had been passed . . . *Dirk Trevallack and Mrs Quintan are safe and well but will be contacting the Consul later in the week, probably on Saturday morning, 2 January.*

'Better get your sleep,' Lievenow said. 'You've got the morning, haven't you?'

The tension relaxed as rapidly as it had blown up. This volatile crew, now that they knew they were not to be betrayed, went out of their way to be pleasant for the rest of the voyage. The weather eased and by midnight on Tuesday, the twenty-ninth, they had cleared the island of Antikithera and were rounding up for the Ionian Sea and the Straits of Otranto. The skipper kept *Kaso* out of sight of land and by Wednesday, as the routine of watch-keeping installed itself, time began to slide by. *Kaso* passed through the Straits during Thursday night and, except for sighting Pelagosa island, she remained deep-sea until Lievenow took her into the Gulf of Venice.

It was dark when the caique finally rounded up for Trieste. The harbour entrance hove into sight beneath the flashing beacons on the breakwaters. Sails furled and chugging rhythmically across the black waters of the immense harbour, *Kaso* slid quietly stern-first on to the eastern jetty. Inconspicuous amongst the fishing boats, Paulos quietly slid the gangway across to the quay. A lorry without lights slid silently from the shadows.

Lievenow shook hands. Paulos kissed Kim on both cheeks. Dirk took her arm and, haversacks slung across their backs, the two English tourists moved off into the night.

Chapter 5

They had spent the rest of the early hours of Saturday morning catching fitful sleep on the benches in the waiting-room of Trieste station. The cold had prevented them oversleeping, so at six they had strengthened themselves with cups of black coffee and hunks of bread in the brasserie on the main-line platform. Things seemed better but their reaction was to put as many kilometres behind them as possible, away from this frontier city. It was too risky to ring London and they made up their minds to move further into Italy as swiftly as they could. The buses assembled outside the station entrance, so they boarded a coach giving its destination as Treviso, in the centre of the Veneto plain, which they reached at 12.20. They found a two-star hotel, The Treviata, in the central square.

'We'll take a couple of rooms to sort ourselves out – and you can have a good night's sleep,' Dirk said.

She could not fathom this man. Brusque to the point of rudeness, yet there were moments when he was almost human. He had brought her all this way, yet there were few signs that his relationship with her had softened to any degree. He certainly had had the opportunities to try his luck, but he had put up an impenetrable barrier – almost as if he was afraid of her. Perhaps the artificial chip-on-her-shoulder she had adopted was the cause of the coldness between them. The sooner the codes were handed to some authority, the happier she would be. She would wish him well and her heart could find solace again in its numbed solitude. With so many dollars in their pockets, they decided to eat well. They lunched in the hotel, then phoned London.

It had been a relief to be able to talk reasonably freely with Henderson and when Dirk emerged from the telephone booth he seemed a different man.

'Two cognacs,' he ordered. 'At last, we know what we've got to do. Henderson is mighty relieved to know where we are and that the codes are safe. Pass me your maps, Kim. He's ringing back in half an hour with more details. He reckons Austria is the safest place to hand over the codes. Have we a map?'

What did he expect? A walking Baedeker? She climbed to her feet and picked up her bag. 'Stay with the things,' she snapped. 'I'll go out and buy one.'

The search for the map took ten minutes, by which time her irritation had simmered down.

'Here you are: the Italian and Austrian borders, Switzerland and Austria, right up to Bavaria and Czechoslovakia.' He spread the map out on the table. As they were orientating themselves, the tinkle of the phone bell rang at the reception desk.

The call was the most difficult they yet had experienced. The line was bad and much had to be repeated. Dirk was sweating when finally they emerged from the kiosk, notes and names and dates scribbled along the sides of the map.

'Phew! What do you make of that?'

'I couldn't catch all Henderson said, but it's a bit of a tall order, isn't it?' Kim complained. 'We're only bank employees, after all.'

He rounded on her. 'What the hell? You're not thinking of giving up now, are you – just when we're almost there?'

His eyes blazed and she caught the disgust in his face. She laid her hand on the sleeve of his jacket, but he pulled his arm away. 'I'm tired, desperately tired –' was all she could say. He left her with her thoughts for a moment, then began to tell her of Henderson's orders.

The Director of the Foreign Division had been adamant about the risk of public transport, and particularly of the railways and airlines. He had contacted the Foreign Office which had, through its agencies, learned of the alerting of Interpol and, yesterday, of the interest of an Arab organization, ACLA, in the flight of the two bank employees from the Lebanon. The Action Commando of the Liberation Army were to be taken very seriously indeed, Henderson said. It was they who had carried out the worst of the international atrocities recently and they were taking the Beirut incident as an insult to their cause. With the money at their disposal, they had built up an enormous agency in Europe. It was rumoured that they were even considering linking up with the Mafia, if, by so doing, the merger could help the Palestinian cause.

Milan and Rome were centres of intrigue in the international espionage systems. Would it not be easier, Henderson asked, now that Trevallack was at Treviso, to cross into Austria? Only seventy miles away, wasn't it? As it happened, the director had explained, the British Bank was sending its President to the EEC conference on a common European currency. This assembly of Europe's leading private bankers was being held in a small Austrian village called Schreck, a few miles north of St Jakob in the Austrian Tyrol. Henderson had checked on his own maps and Schreck could not be more than a hundred miles from Treviso as the crow flew.

'Why don't you deliver OEDIPUS to Mr Donald McHuish personally? Then everyone will know that the codes are safe, because the bank is running its own courier service and security from Schreck.'

'Suits me,' Dirk had replied spontaneously. 'Anything to get rid of the bloody things,' and Henderson had laughed down the line. He had proceeded to offer detailed planning: the conference was not due to start until late January, the opening ceremony being on Wednesday, 27 January – barely three weeks ahead. Dirk was to go to Schreck as soon as possible, where he was to report to one of the consortium's staff, Antony Rice, the bank's communications expert. Rice was being instructed to contact London as soon as Dirk had reported and Dirk was to meet Rice daily. If anything went wrong, whilst waiting for Mr McHuish to arrive in Schreck, the bank would then know at once. Dirk could discharge his trust as soon as the President arrived.

'Time is not so important as security, Trevallack,' Henderson had emphasized. 'Don't forget you're being hunted for the theft of the bank's cash and securities – that's officially what the authorities are chasing you for.' The line became very bad and there seemed to be some cross-connections. Half a minute elapsed before Henderson came back again. '. . . that you, Trevallack? Yes, Henderson here. D'you get all that? Adequate funds? Good. We're very pleased here. You're saving us millions. Take care.'

There had been nothing else and the call was terminated briskly.

'So here we are, Kim,' Dirk said, taking her arm. 'Let's go upstairs and sort this mess out.'

He took her straight to his room and locked the door behind them. She spread the map across his bed and together they began to piece together the journey which lay before them.

She liked his incisiveness as he weighed up all the snags, and tried to forestall the problems that this final phase of their journey would possibly bring. Beneath Dirk's hard exterior, she was sure that what was concerning him most was the chore of having to drag her along with him. She could, she realized suddenly, leave him now, if she was really a burden to him.

'Dirk,' she said quietly as she sat by him on the bed. 'I want to complete this thing with you.' She suddenly placed her hands on either side of his face and forced him to face her. 'You're a bit of a martyr about everything; if I'm an encumbrance to you, I can easily return home to England independently. I'd be safer on my own, in a way.' She had not meant the *double entendre*, but he had not noticed. Instead, he gently prised off her hands and told her not to be a fool.

'You stupid girl,' he said. 'I need you. Reckon we may be needing our skis too, if Henderson's warnings are anything to go by. Look here . . .' and he smoothed off the map again to trace their route with his finger. 'If we get to Trento, we could catch a bus up to Bressanone. There might even be a coach to Lienz and Klagenfurt. We could drop off about here, if the frontier is being watched. It would be easy enough to ski over the border, without any questions asked. It's good to see that Italian stamp on the passports, though, isn't it? If we have as little difficulty with them as we had at Trieste, there's not much to worry about.' He looked up at her then and for the first time she realized that he was not being critical. He patted her hand. 'We started this together. Let's finish it.'

'I won't bring the subject up again. Just hope I don't hold you back, that's all.'

'Shut up and let's get on with the planning. We'll buy some warm ski clothes and sleep here tonight.'

He allowed her to take his arm, while they walked down Treviso's main street in search of a sports shop. He seemed in high spirits with the thought of positive action.

They took nearly two hours to choose their clothes. She needed his approval and after the first shyness had passed, he joined in the game. They looked the part now – earnest English, off to the resorts.

After supper in the hotel, they went up to their floor together. She was wondering throughout the meal whether he would try anything. Pushing the thought behind her, she was, she told herself, relieved that they parted in the corridor.

'Good night,' he said brusquely. 'We'll make an early start. Give me a shake, will you?' He opened the door for her and she slipped inside. After he had pulled it shut, she heard him passing down the passage. She leaned for a moment against the door, her thoughts in a strange turmoil.

She turned the key slowly in the lock.

Chapter 6

The first bus left at 7.45 on the next morning, Sunday, 3 January, but the two British skiers had to change at Citadella for Trento. After Bassano, the route followed the course of the Brenta river until Grigno, where the road began snaking into the mountains. They passed the lake at Levico, finally reaching Trento at 3.30. On a Sunday afternoon, the Italian bus company offered little promise of transport to Lienz until late on Monday morning; strikes and snow conditions were badly affecting services.

'A couple of pizzas is what we need,' Dirk said, and led the way into the bar next to the booking office. The food put new heart into them and the depression began to evaporate. Even if Henderson had discouraged the railways, the train was the only means of reaching Austria rapidly, apart from hiring a car.

'Too expensive and apart from that, there's the frontier road to think about,' Kim said. 'Keep off the focal points, Mr Henderson said, didn't he?'

Trento station was in need of its first redecoration since its modernization. The paint was peeling off the doors of the waiting-rooms and some panes of glass were cracked.

They found the waiting-room and dumped their gear on a vacant bench and tried to sleep. They spent the long hours, talking and getting to know each other better than they ever had during these past two years. Dirk was losing the antipathy he had felt for her: she seemed less critical of him and was accepting his leadership now. The enforced proximity was breaking down the barriers and he was beginning to feel at ease with her. His fear was that she would be unable to keep up the pace, now that they were on the last lap.

'It's 10.55,' Kim said. 'No. 2 platform, isn't it?'

He took the bulk of the gear, while she dealt with the tickets. As they lined up at the barrier, two men emerged from behind one of the pillars. They were each carrying a bag and were heavily coated against the cold. The taller of the two wore a black astrakhan, the other a peaked Glengarry, and even in this sombre lighting, they both wore dark glasses. They were in their thirties, but by their silence remained aloof from the other travellers. Dirk did not care for the look of them and was relieved when they walked on ahead after reaching the platform. He was becoming jittery in the role he was being forced to play . . . the whole incident was ridiculous. Kim was scrutinizing the tickets: *wagon* 26, berths 59 and 60.

They passed the massive diesel engine with its concertinaed conductor mast stowed on the roof. The whole train, except for the rear portion in which *wagon* 26 found itself, was built of shining, fluted aluminium. It was an impressive sight with the engine's livery of silver blue.

The man was nodding wisely. '*Douane*, yes,' and stuffing the passports into his file, he shuffled down the corridor to meet his next bunch of passengers. Dirk entered the *wagon-lit* and closed the door behind him.

The compartment was modernly equipped. On the engine side were two bunks, one above the other, clean in their tartan blankets and white sheets. Opposite the door was the wash-basin and cabinet. Two glasses in hygienic polythene wrappings were stacked in holders on the wall. Underneath, when Dirk opened the lower cupboard, was a large chamber pot. He closed the door, but he saw that she was trying not to laugh.

'Well, Mrs Quintan . . . ?'

'Yes, Mr Trevallack?' And she placed her hand naturally on his sleeve. 'If I need that during the night, I promise you I'll use the lavatory.'

'Seriously, though, if we run into trouble, we'd better act as man and wife, or at least . . .'

'It'd look a bit odd if we didn't,' and she chuckled, as she searched for the perfume bottle in her bag. She was trying to unpack the few things she had brought with her, but she was taking a long time about it. 'I'm dying to sleep again in a nightie,' she said. 'Perhaps I can buy one the next time we reach civilization?'

'I'll smoke one of my last cigars,' he said. He foraged in his haversack, then went out into the corridor and stood outside the lavatory. There was too much of a draught for his match, so he edged to the open side and crouched downwards, cupping his hands. As the match was flaring, two men shoved past him.

'Restaurant?' the first asked, in broken English. Dirk recognized them as the mysterious pair in the station. The taller repeated the question and Dirk pointed towards the front of the train. 'It's only a bar. . . . Snacks, perhaps.' He caught the smaller man's eyes, but they passed on without a word.

Dirk drew deeply on his cigar. Nasty looking couple – they'd slit their grandmother's throat, by the looks of them – and he braced himself against the swaying of the train which was now rocking along through the dark night. The pleasure of this Dutch cigar was giving him time to think.

Kim and he were becoming used to each other – she was good to have around. A silent truce existed; for two days she had not used the sarcasm he had found so childish at the bank. He had really put her through it these last few days, but she had complained only once – and then with every reason. He had a premonition that, though they were entering the last phase of OEDIPUS, they were not through the wood yet – and he felt again beneath his shirt for the codes wrapped around him. The train was slowing down for the suburbs of Bolzano which were flashing past the window. He returned to the *wagon-lit*, where Kim was tucked into her bunk.

'Bolzano,' he said. 'They divide the train here.'

A bare arm reached up for the light, the circle of her hair a vivid red on the pillow. She had pulled the blanket up to her chin and she seemed a young girl as she smiled shyly up at him, her hazel eyes shining and flecked with emerald. The train decelerated and then an Italian voice was gabbling through the platform loud-speakers: passengers for Lienz and Klagenfurt must be in the rear portion of the train. '*Attentione* . . . the front portion of the Innsbruck express moves off in two minutes.'

They felt the tremor as the train was uncoupled and then Dirk went into the corridor to watch the coupling up of their new loco-motive. He pulled down a fraction of the window. The cold was intense and his eyes began running. He heard the clanging of a hand-bell as the guard signalled the engine on to the buffers of the last coach. They were coupling up two locomotives, one at each end: it must be a climb up to the pass. He turned his head to peer for-wards. The red light on the rear of the Innsbruck section was disappearing into the night. The lead engine and several new carriages were sliding towards the remainder of the train, while another bell-ringing official was directing the driver. From a doorway, three coaches up, three men were descending to the platform.

From the corner of his window, Dirk watched the group huddled in conversation. The controller was in the centre, gesticulating with his hands, as he indicated the length of the train; he was shrugging his shoulders in opposition to the other two whom Dirk had no difficulty in recognizing. The larger was prodding the controller's chest and the little man in the gold braid took exception and stomped off down the platform. They followed after him, like a pair of beagles. The train jolted again and the new front portion was coupled up.

Dirk could stand the cold no longer. His breath steamed in the night air and his ears were already numb. The loudspeakers blared again and three minutes later the train slid from the station. The illuminated clock was showing 11.57 – the Bolzano–Klagenfurt stopping train was punctual to the minute.

Kim was turned away from him when he closed the door behind him. She was smaller than he had realized, curled up beneath the blankets. The girl was worn out, so he would not bother her with his suspicions. Dawn would arrive soon enough or he could put her in the picture when they reached Dobbiaco – the customs people would be bound to wake them up. He slipped out of his trousers and hung them with his anorak on one of the hooks. He hauled himself into his upper bunk and lay on his back for a few moments, his hands beneath his head, waiting for sleep to overtake him as he turned over the suspicions running through his mind. He felt uneasy, like a hunted stag must feel when scenting for the first time the hounds on the far side of Dunkery Beacon. He used to follow the hunt when his father took them up to Exmoor – and the memories flooded back. His imagination used to work overmuch and his sympathies, even as a child, were always with the magnificent beast they were about to hound to death; and now he felt the same horror crowding in upon him. And he had dragged a woman in to all this. So far, this flight had been a game, but if they were now the quarry for men of the calibre he had seen on the platform, he had better watch his step. Kim and he were too vulnerable – not even armed. He reached over the bunk and hauled his knife from the pocket of his trousers.

'What's worrying you?'

Her voice spoke quietly from the gloom of the blue lighting beneath his bunk. She had been awake, feigning sleep – or had he woken her?

'Those evil-looking men, that couple we first saw when we were buying our tickets – they're on the train.'

'On our section, the Lienz–Klagenfurt half?'

'I've just spotted them again. They were checking up with the controller of our carriage. It looked as if they were asking him to search the train.'

'Police?'

'Plain clothes men, more likely.'

'Probably looking for smugglers,' Kim said. 'These frontiers must be notorious for the currency racket.'

'You're right. The coincidence is much too absurd, but I've got this feeling and I can't shake it off.' Then he remembered the interruption and the interference during Henderson's call: the sudden break, the reconnection. He remained silent.

' 'Night, Kim.'

'. . . umm, sleep well.' She sounded deliciously sleepy, too tired to talk.

'Kim? You awake?'

'Uh-huh.'

'You undressed?'

There was silence, then a sharpness in her voice: 'Not entirely.'

Again the long silence. What the hell made a woman tick . . .? She murmured something, but he did not catch her words.

'What is it then?' She was angry, damn her eyes.

'Reckon we should sleep dressed tonight,' he said.

'Worried?' She still sounded irritated as she snapped on the light.

'If someone is really after us, we might have to quit fast.' The train was drawing up at the first station. He drew back the lip of the curtain: *Chiusa*. He glanced across at the map on the compartment wall. It was thirteen kilometres to Bressanone, then eight to the fork where the line divided: straight on for Innsbruck; and Lienz, thirty-four kilometres to the east, inside the Austrian border.

'So that's what you meant,' she said quietly.

By the time the train had reached Bressanone, they had dressed again. Kim was back in bed, but she had thrown off a blanket. If they had to leave in a hurry, she had only to slip into her anorak, grab her woolly hat, haversack and grip. He would take the rest.

The train was swerving off to the eastward as it followed the course of the Isarco river. Dirk felt the speed decreasing as the engines began working up the gradient. Vandoies came next but, judging by her snores, Kim was well away. Drowsiness overcame him as they slid into Brunico just before two o'clock. The train must have waited there for some time, for he never remembered its departure. Monguelfo was twenty-one kilometres further on . . .

He slept fitfully, the bunk hard beneath his hip. . . . He felt a gentle pressure on his shoulder, and woke with a start. For an instant, lost to his whereabouts.

'Are you awake?' she whispered. 'There's a lot of coming-and-going in the corridor.'

He scrambled from his bunk, swung to the floor. She lay on her bunk watching him, a blanket thrown loosely around her. He delved beneath her bunk, searching for his new snow boots.

He sat on the edge of her bed. In the corridor, several men were talking; he recognized the voice of the controller.

'You look very suspicious, fully dressed,' she whispered. 'If it's customs, what are you going to say?'

Before he had time to answer, there was a tap on the door.

'Dobbiaco,' the controller's voice called. '*Douane*, Signor, signora . . .' and the catch on the door began to rattle. The train was drawing into Dobbiaco station.

'Quick,' Kim whispered. She snapped out the light and threw back the bedclothes. She opened her arms to him, pulled him alongside her and flung the blanket across them. She pressed his head into her shoulder, laying her hand across his cheek, as the door slowly opened. He felt the heat of her body and then she was kissing him as the controller stood in the doorway.

'Signor, signora. *Douane*. . . . The man switched on the main light.

Dirk half-turned from the woman's arms, blinking in the light. 'What the hell d'you want?'

'Anything to declare, sir?' an Austrian customs *politzei* was demanding in his guttural English. 'Where are you going, pliss?' He was taking his time in scrutinizing the passports, his shrewd eyes checking the details. An imperceptible glance passed between the two officials and then the peak-capped, green-uniformed *politzei* spoke rapidly in German. He nodded, glanced at the embarrassed couple and saluted briefly as he handed the passports back to the Italian controller.

'Passports, please,' Dirk said brusquely. He could feel the anger mounting inside him. The Austrian policeman and the controller

42

were playing with them. The Italian grinned and slowly handed the documents across.

'Thanks.'

The *politzei* backed away, his eyes travelling swiftly over the haversacks. He said nothing, but switched off the light and closed the door. The compartment was once more in darkness.

He lay there motionless, her arm about him. Her softness and the warmth of her was sweeping over him, but he gently disengaged himself. She sat up as he left the bunk. The train was moving off again and through the chink in the blind he could see the station lights of Dobbiaco sliding past. On the platform stood a bunch of Italian and Austrian police stamping their feet; their breath was steaming in the freezing air as they laughed and shook hands. The train gathered speed and the green-coated Austrians swung themselves into a carriage at the rear.

'I don't like this a bit,' Dirk said. 'Perhaps it's normal to have so many police at the frontier but . . .' He slipped their passports into a pocket of the haversacks as Kim flipped the bolt across the door.

'They're coming back,' she whispered.

He heard them then, their boots heavy on the alloy plating of the corridor. The controller's voice was clearly distinguishable as they approached but, as they came abreast *wagon-lits* 59 and 60, conversation ceased. The sound of their footsteps disappeared as they moved up the corridor, towards the front of the train.

'There were three or four,' Dirk said. 'They'll start at the front, while their buddies begin searching from the rear.'

The train was slowing down – and then he felt the coach lurch to the right. Through the slit in the blind, he could see the train moving slowly into a loop siding. Large, carmine-tinged snow flakes were falling like thistle-down. A red signal glowed at the entrance to a tunnel.

'We're waiting for the westbound train, I suppose. This can be only single track through the tunnel.' He glanced at the map on the wall opposite him.

'Look, Kim. . . . We're equidistant with Sillian. We must be very close to the frontier. There's bound to be another check on the other side.' He could feel the net enveloping them. They could either sit here hoping or . . .

He jumped up, grabbed the haversacks. 'We're baling out.'

She picked up her share. He slid back the catch on the door. The corridor blazed with light, but was empty. He moved swiftly towards the front of the carriage. Three yards only and they had reached the space outside the lavatory. They stood by the exit door which opened on to the off-side track. Kim was tugging at his sleeve.

'They're coming back.'

The connecting door from the adjacent carriage was opening.

'Into the loo . . .'

He yanked open the door and pulled her after him. He flicked the lock to engaged. Lights flashed past the frosted glass as the down-express rumbled past. He heard the voice of the controller passing down the corridor, perhaps to their compartment. Their Lienz train shuddered, began rolling forwards.

'Stay close to me,' he whispered. 'We're getting out.'

He eased out of the lavatory, then grabbed the handle of the carriage door which rotated inwards on its axis. He grabbed Kim and swung her into the darkness, clear of the accelerating train. He balanced on the step and pulled shut the carriage door behind him. Protecting his head with his disengaged arm, he leapt into the void.

Chapter 7

'You okay, Dirk?'

He had fallen badly. The train had been moving faster than he realized. He could see Kim's silhouette against the faint half-moon of the tunnel entrance. She was bending over him, worried, trying to bring him to his senses. No broken bones, no sprains. . . . She helped him to his feet, then pointed to the green signal light reflecting from the arch of the tunnel.

'Can't hear our train any more,' she said. 'D'you think they spotted us?'

'Certain they didn't. They'll have to search the length of the train. I slammed the door behind me.'

'We ought to clear out of here,' she said. 'The next train from Lienz may be coming this way soon.'

As he picked up the haversacks, a red glow bathed the tunnel mouth – the east–west train was on its way. He felt a pressure on his ear drums and then the vibration on the rails. He took her hand and pulled her towards the tunnel exit. He stuck his head cautiously round the corner of the brickwork.

It was snowing hard, the large flakes tumbling downwards to fashion a white veil across the mouth of the tunnel. He could see only a few yards, but a yellow glow from the platform lights glimmered ahead. There was no sign of the Italian police. He heard the rumble of the train behind them, its hooter blaring. As he emerged into the snowstorm, he crossed through the green pool of light thrown by the signal above them. He tugged Kim after him and moved off down the tracks of the loop siding.

They stood motionless as the train slid past them, the dim lighting from its coaches casting an eerie glow in the falling snow. The brakes creaked, the buffers of the carriages slammed and the train halted. A loudspeaker was crackling from the platform: '*Dobbiaco . . . Dobbiaco . . .*'

'Quick. Through this gate . . . '

Shielded from the platform by the waiting train, they scrambled through the snow. He pushed open the spring-loaded barrier, held it for her, then passed through the goods yard. Several cars were parked behind the delivery vans, but the yard was empty of life.

Dobbiaco was surprisingly busy at this early hour. Though it was only 5·30, the mail vans were already setting out on their rounds and people were scurrying to work. Dirk and Kim entered a sleepy café where workmen were downing their coffees before facing another day. The two itinerant skiers elicited no interest. When they had swallowed their frothy *espressos*, they followed the general exodus to the autocar station. By six o'clock, the bus was on its way, down the road in the direction from which they had come in the train. Twenty-five minutes later they were at Monguelfo; at 7·10 in the bus terminus.

The flush of dawn was touching the mountain ranges to the eastward. The fast-running river was dark and mysterious where it coursed beneath its snow-covered ice, beneath the bridge in the centre of the town.

'We'll stop here,' Dirk said. 'Breakfast. We've got to decide what to do next.'

The food and the warmth put new heart into them and they studied their map. The Austrian border was only fifteen kilometres from the village of Limouro which lay in the valley, sixteen kilometres to the north. When Dirk asked the café proprietor about the chances of finding accommodation there, he was surprised at the beaming smile: Limouro was one of the villages rapidly building its reputation as a *langlauf* centre. The snob resorts could boast their Alpine skiing, but the sport of ski-touring was catching on rapidly throughout the minor resorts.

By 10·30 they were striding along the road for Limouro and for three and a half hours they climbed up a narrow, ice-covered lane winding into the mountains. They left the snow-laden woods behind them, then passed through the pine forests. They finally emerged on to a desolate open valley, but overhead the sky was cloudless blue, now that the snow had passed. White cascades, their icy poniards frozen in mid-descent, hung from the precipices bordering the road. Everywhere, nature continued its remorseless process of destruction and re-animation. Then, round the corner of the track carved from the mountainside, they came upon the first sign of habitation, an ancient farmhouse chalet tucked into the shelter of the mountain.

Limouro was a typical Italian hamlet, its few chalets huddled together for mutual protection when the weather was bad. The only road ran down the centre and the chalets, their backs buried deep in the snow, were like picture postcards on this early afternoon. It was already 1·20 and Kim and he were ravenous. There was a baker and a food shop, but apart from the chemist situated aloofly on a small rise, there seemed to be no inn or hotel. A painted board extolling Limouro as a ski-touring centre faced them and, on the other side of the road, an address board announced the whereabouts of the principal houses.

No hotels, no inns, but plenty of *pensions* . . . and then, at the bottom, a larger board, its white background painted over in bright blue letters: *Holiday Colony and Ski School, 400 metres.*

'Are you game?' he asked her. Having walked the sixteen kilometres without protest, he was expecting some complaining. Without a murmur she led off up the road, her small figure bowed in front of him as she leaned against the weight of her pack. The road curled to the right and disappeared into the darkness of a clump of pines. A modern, chalet-style building stood on the slope. The ski-school was built in the modern idiom, its main structure being off-centre. Its accompanying wing sloped to the right, its low-pitched roof in handsome proportion relative to the house.

It was warm inside, warm with friendliness and central heating . . . and of course the English were welcome here. Signor Luigi Todaro was produced from his office, a genial Italian of about thirty-five. He could speak good English, one of the qualifications which had earned him his appointment, because each year more Britons were discovering Limouro and its holiday colony.

'What are your charges?' Dirk asked diffidently.

'What you can afford, signor – one of the rules of the centre.' He smiled at the disbelief of his visitors. 'Pay for your food, that's all our Society asks. We help children from all over Italy. If you wish to take part in our life here, we should be very happy.'

'How many children have you here at the moment?' Kim asked, her taut face softening.

'120, from all walks of life. Some from broken homes and others with psychological problems. I shouldn't be too enthusiastic, if I were you – you may want to leave tomorrow. I'll save some lunch for you. Let me show you to your rooms . . .'

Kim had already dropped the hint, so there were no difficulties over accommodation. They were taken upstairs and shown to rooms 36 and 37, on opposite sides of the corridor running the length of the wing. Dirk dumped his gear in the narrow room. He would deposit the cash and the securities with the Director, but would continue to conceal the codes about his person. Kim was tapping on the door.

Soup, mountains of sauerkraut and a platter of local cheeses, put them back on top. By the time they had savoured the coffee which the beaming Italian girl brought them, they had made their decision. They would stay until Dirk was proficient enough at ski-touring to make the trip across the frontier into Austria. The Director who had joined them at their table, could introduce them to a guide.

After a briefing by Luigi Todaro, they walked down to the village to prepare for the strenuous days ahead. The towering range of the Hohe Tauern stretched across the horizon, black in the gathering darkness. The route through those mountains led into Austria and, according to Todaro, the two-day trip was not difficult.

They passed the ski-shop, its brightly lit window one of the few attractions in the village. A range of *langlauf* skis was displayed, tempting in their slender elegance.

'Todaro said he can fix us up with skis. If I get on all right and you can show me how to cope, we'll equip ourselves,' Dirk said.

'You don't know what you are letting yourself in for.' Kim's curt reaction surprised him. 'Downhill skiing is child's play in comparison.' She went on, 'You have to know your mountains if you want to tour – and survive. Though you have to recognize all the signs, the snow conditions and the weather, I'm certain that instinct plays the greatest part.'

Dirk was trying once again to fathom the enigma of this slender woman. She was waxing vehemently on the joys of ski-touring. Her hazel eyes flashed and a half-smile was playing at the corners of her mouth.

'Where d'you learn all this stuff?' he asked, as they walked on. She paused, momentarily embarrassed by her animated spiel.

'I met my ex-husband when ski-mountaineering and I lost my heart to the sport. There were some wonderful guides in Switzerland and they taught me all I know – which isn't much. The guide is like the sailor – he respects the element with which he works. He's never afraid of postponing a tour if he has doubts about the weather. If conditions are ripe for avalanches, he takes every possible precaution. He doesn't have to prove anything: he's seen too many tragedies.'

They walked back to the chalet and were glad to get out of the bitter cold. Supper was a happy, noisy affair. Some hundred youngsters from thirteen to twenty years old, sat at their long wooden tables, chattering with excitement as they relived the day. There were few adults, but there was a sense of discipline beneath the happiness that reigned here. The racket subsided as the children dispersed to their rooms.

'Bed,' Kim said. 'Sleep is what you want, sir, if you want to cross those mountains.'

He followed her upstairs and escorted her to her room. In the morning they would equip themselves with the centre's skis and gear.

'What time shall I call you?' she asked, hesitating at her door.

'Breakfast's at 7·30.'

'Seven, then?'

'Thanks.'

' 'Night.' She slowly closed the door upon him.

He stood motionless for a moment, then crossed to his room. Too tired to sleep, the thoughts revolved through his mind. Was it worth the risk, trying to safeguard the bank's interest by crossing those mountains? He had his own life to consider, but what about Kim Quintan's? She was an obstinate girl who would never give up. This was one of the dangers; the other was that as she stood at her door tonight, for the first time, he was thinking of her as a woman – and an attractive one, at that.

Chapter 8

Dirk spent the first day, Tuesday, 5 January, trying to master the new techniques. He found the action more difficult than he had supposed and by the end of the day he was nearly crippled. The long stride, the shove with the long sticks, and the raising of the heel as he strode forwards – all was strange, after downhill skiing.

As they walked slowly back to the ski-room that evening, she could see the disappointment in his face. He was persevering, but *langlaufing* was not coming naturally to him. The grace and rhythm of the born ski-tourer were certainly eluding Mr Trevallack at the moment. He was holding the door open, having taken her skis.

'I'll never make it,' he said quietly. 'I'm walking and picking up my skis, instead of gliding along. We'll have to find some other way of getting across.'

'Don't worry. Once you've got hold of the basics, you'll make progress. I was just the same.'

'These bloody codes . . .' and then he shut up like a clam.

That night he was withdrawn from the others. He was morose and was making no effort to share the interests of the evening. 'I'm whacked,' he whispered to her at the end of the meal. 'I'm off to bed.' She watched him hauling himself up the stone stairway. His shoulders were stooped and the red stockings were wrinkled about his calves. His hair was dishevelled and his face was grey with tiredness.

Kim Quintan recognized the danger signals in herself. She wanted to mother him, to take care of that overgrown boy. She quietly left the table to find a corner seat on the settle in the hall. She could be at peace here in Limouro; she could try to unscramble the feelings struggling inside her. She had not felt these stirrings for years and she felt disturbed. No one had dared to draw back the curtains she had cast about herself. She was not sure whether she wanted him to try. She rose from the settle and slowly climbed the stairs.

There was no light beneath his doorway. He must be asleep already. She tip-toed past and silently opened the door of her room. She too was exhausted. The sleep she craved would submerge these forgotten longings.

Wednesday dawned, with sunlight. The beginners' course, under the tutelage of Rossi, their instructor and guide, began to make progress. Kim stayed with them: she could help with the duffers and she did not want to leave Dirk. The class made its first tour up a forest track and back across the hilltop to the chalet.

'It's a damn sight more difficult coming down than climbing up,' Dirk said with his rare smile. 'I'm still not used to walking straight up the full-line of a slope.'

The week slipped past: blue skies and sun, good snow and the days becoming longer. By Sunday, 10 January, Dirk was gaining his confidence.

'At least, I can keep up with Rossi,' he told her as they stepped from their skis at the end of the day. 'He's taking us on a twenty-kilometre tour tomorrow.'

She took his hand. It was good, this developing friendship. Their shyness was disappearing and he was more natural with her.

'We'll make the mountains yet,' she told him.

By Thursday the fourteenth, Dirk was enjoying the sport. Each morning and afternoon was spent on longer runs and, by the end of that week, they were up on the glacier and taking their haversacks with them. On the following Sunday the seventeenth, they and five others were sitting in the sun on a patch of barren, wind-swept rock. Limouro was a toy hamlet, seven hundred metres below.

'I know what you meant now,' Dirk said. 'This takes a lot of beating.'

She was at peace. The solitude of this shining world was the magnet which drew her into the mountains.

The group was silent as it munched the sandwiches and sipped the sweet lemonade. Rossi, his rope coiled about him and his alpenstock stuck into his knapsack, sat apart, his eyes absorbing everything about them. The clouds, the wind, the texture of the snow – he missed nothing, alert to the slightest change. An avalanche on the Hohe Tauern had claimed his father three years earlier. Rossi and three others had been the only survivors out of a party of nine. He never mentioned the tragedy, but when he talked of snow craft, his voice was a listless monotone.

Kim allowed the sun and the tranquillity to seep into her, as she leaned against Dirk's shoulder. She closed her eyes, the fire from the sun, a crimson mist beneath her closed lids. A breeze whispered across the crest as wisps of powder snow spiralled in minuscule whirlwinds across the snowfields stretching down to the valleys below. For eighty kilometres, the mountain ranges stretched white before her, the tips of the highest peaks jutting into the cold cerulean of this cold, clear day. Behind her snaked the Austrian frontier, two thousand metres higher, but only ten kilometres away, Rossi said. The summit of Gross Venediger thrust into the blue to the north of them, while to the eastwards, Gross Glockner, over four thousand metres high, completed the symmetry of the crescent forming the Hohe Tauern. Somewhere between those peaks, nestling in a concealed valley was the village of Schreck, their objective.

'Rossi will introduce us to a guide tonight,' Dirk said quietly. 'An experienced bloke named Emmanuel Berlini who knows the route well. If we start early, we need spend only one night on the way. There's a hut called the Chamois specially there for the tourers.'

'Does he approve of your trying this trip?'

She was sure he was hiding something from her. For her part, she could stay here for ever. Lost to the world, living simply and helping Dirk as unobtrusively as she could, was all that she asked of life at this moment. He was staring across her, to the valley below.

'Rossi's happy about my skiing,' he was saying. 'Another few days and I'll be fit enough to have a go, provided Berlini will take us.'

He hesitated, silent again. Her curls were escaping beneath her red hat as the breeze tugged at her hair.

'You'll come, Kim? Over the mountains?'

He turned and faced her. His face was burned and a stubble of beard was beginning to show. The party had foregathered at six this morning.

She laid her mitt on the sleeve of his anorak: 'Provided the guide is happy about us. . . .' She could see the relief in his eyes. The responsibility of their secret commission was wearing him down. Schreck so near but yet so far, with those mountains barring the way – and these were merely the foothills to the Alps. Rossi, too, had said that the Schreck run was simple enough: there was only one difficult section, the climb to the Chamois hut at three thousand five hundred metres. After that, the long run down was easy . . .

Their instructor was on his feet and preparing for the afternoon's return to Limouro. His eyes darted everywhere and he seemed unhappy about the long traverse of the snowfields above the glacier. He led off in silence, insisting that each followed precisely in the other's track. This season had been an exceptionally cold winter, with more snow than anyone could remember since the terrible winter of '50–'51 when more snow had fallen than in any winter in living memory. A sudden rise in temperature had followed a prolonged blizzard. For days, avalanches had thundered throughout the Alps.

The villagers still talked of that year – entire communities had been swept away by the *lawines*. Kim glanced upwards as the party moved off. Slabs of grey clouds were moving in from the south, lower than for many days The peaks of Venediger and Glockner were already donning their grey mantles. She shivered and tucked her scarf deeper into her anorak.

Dirk was several metres ahead of her, going well now. She followed exactly in his tracks, the hiss of the powder snow music to her ears. The snow crystals glistened like diamonds. The air bit into her face as they swung across the gigantic snow field. She sensed the tension in the party: too many skiers had been lost by acting irresponsibly off the runs. But with Rossi they were safe.

Their guide was smiling when finally they reached the village at dusk. He would be expecting all his class in the 'Rosa', the bar which Dirk had used on their first evening. It had been a good day. The challenge they had experienced had bonded the party together to a remarkable degree.

After supper, Kim and Dirk left the holiday chalet to its own devices. She had taken time over her make-up and when she took Dirk's arm she experienced a long-forgotten exhilaration. They slithered down to the 'Rosa' and judging by the noise of the singing escaping through the shutters, the party was already well away. Rossi had insisted that his class must celebrate its dispersal in traditional Limouro style.

Inside, all was smoke, warmth and laughter. The three-man group of accordion, drummer and guitarist were bashing out a beat to which the packed room was dancing. Rossi and his friends, the guides and instructors of Limouro, had formed a circle and, arms about each other's shoulders, were singing with rollicking gusto. She hesitated with Dirk on the edge of the room, but then Rossi saw them. With a cry of welcome, he threw his arms about Kim's waist, kissed her fully on the lips, then hauled her over to a table where a solitary man was sitting. He was dragging at a long, thin cigar, whilst watching the antics of the couples cavorting on the floor.

'Signor Berlini,' Rossi introduced in his broken English. 'He speaks a little English.'

Rossi handed them over to this taciturn man and Kim left the talking to Dirk. He was good with people and she watched him with amusement as he tried to sum up the elderly guide who would be holding their lives in his hands. She watched them both, the Englishman in his twenties, and the middle-aged, leathery Italian who earned his living the hard way.

Berlini crossed the frontier twice a week, Rossi had said, sometimes with skiers, at others with unknown clients, but often on his own – and if a man of Berlini's calibre took *that* risk, Kim thought, he must be involved in something important or, more probably, illegal. Rossi had talked little about Berlini – the man was a mystery, a loner, by all accounts. But he was, by reputation, one of the best guides in the locality.

'Signor Berlini suggests next Friday, the twenty-second.' Dirk had turned towards her and she noted the question in his glance. 'He wants two hundred pounds in Austrian schillings – half now, and the remainder when he gets us to Schreck.'

She thought quickly, unwilling to hurt his feelings.

'Does he consider we're up to it?'

'He reckons, from what Rossi has told him, that I could benefit from a few more days of toughening up. You're okay.' He smiled at her, but there was no resentment now in his glance. 'Anyway, he can't take us until Friday, because he's got some courier job.'

'Seems reasonable enough to me. The charge won't break BB.'

She watched the large bank notes changing hands as, there and then, Dirk paid Berlini in schillings. There was nothing else that they could do. The balance would be paid when they reached Schreck. The unsmiling Emmanuel picked up his cap and rose to go. Tall and lean, with huge shoulders, he had, he was telling Dirk, been one of the first to introduce ski-touring to this area. Born in Dobbiaco, he knew these mountains like his own backyard. During the summer he tended his cows and the three fields he hired below the pines. In the winter, while his wife looked after the cattle in the stalls at the back of their chalet, he made his living by using his snow craft to better advantage than the instructors with their interminable *langlauf* classes.

54

They shook hands and watched the powerful figure threading his way through the crush to the door. They took the floor and, for the next few hours, danced their feet off. She felt the comfort of his arm about her but the evening was more of a gymnastic exercise than a romantic *entente*. They sat out only once to regain their breath and to sink some of the local wine.

She was content, happier than she had been for years. Friday would arrive all too soon – the codes would be delivered and that would be the end of what, for her, had become an exhilarating adventure. That night, as she lingered at her door, he kissed her lightly on the forehead for the first time. She stood on her toes and returned the compliment on his cheek. He was taking no chances – and nor was she. It was past one o'clock but sleep was a long time in coming for her that night.

Monday and Tuesday brought a break in the weather, but they joined an advanced class touring the adjacent hills. By Tuesday night the blizzard hit the little village, a storm lasting for thirty-six hours. There was nothing that Dirk could do, but to mope in the chalet, frustrated and bad-tempered as he glowered through the windows at the huge flakes driving horizontally against the building outside.

'This will scrub our trip,' he said. 'Berlini will never take us after this.'

At midday on Wednesday the snow had stopped. The sun emerged, the afternoon was warm and the evening brought a clear sky. To her relief, Dirk's morale began to improve. On Thursday, while on the morning's run with Rossi, a message came from Berlini that he would take them as planned, provided the weather held. The report for the area was unsettled, but so long as the wind held from the east, Berlini would start at six. He would meet them outside the holiday chalet so that they could put the easiest part of the journey behind them before dawn broke. They would need every minute of daylight, if they were to reach the Chamois hut before mid-afternoon.

They spent the afternoon checking their gear, discarding the inessentials. Kim insisted that she carried her own haversack. They supped early, collected their bagged lunches, said their goodbyes to the colony and paid up their shares. Luigi and his wife were waiting for them in the hall.

'If Berlini says it's all right,' the Italian said, 'I suppose it must be okay.' He was uncommunicative as he tapped the barometer hanging on the pine-wood wall. He shook his head.

'*Arrivederci*,' he said, holding out his hand. 'Hope to see you again one day.'

As Kim preceded Dirk upstairs, she watched Luigi talking to his wife and shaking his head. Outside, the wind was whining against the shutters.

Chapter 9

He woke at 5·30 and padded across the passage to wake Kim. They went through their check list, perhaps for the last time. The day after tomorrow they would be in Schreck. They slipped through the doors of the chalet. Outside, in the shadows cast by the safety light, Emmanuel Berlini was waiting, the freezing water vapour from his breath forming icicles upon his hat and eyebrows. He shook hands without a word and then they were off to the teleski. Dirk felt elated when the cold hit him. They had made it, and were on the last stage of their journey. He strode after Berlini, then remembered the girl he was taking with him.

'Sorry, Kim. Can't believe we're really off.' He checked once again the wad beneath his shirt. All complete – and now to concentrate on the job in hand.

The teleski crew were waiting for them. The cable operator shook hands with Berlini and passed them on to the youth who was lugging milk and water churns into the cabin for the summit hut which was served daily with fresh supplies. The doors slammed shut, the motors of the winding machines whined and the car slid from beneath the overhanging roof of the station.

'Pity it's dark,' Kim said. 'It's our last look at Limouro.'

'We've been here sixteen days. Henderson would be doing his nut, if we hadn't sent that explanatory telegram.'

They swooped into space, but only a few lights were visible in the village which was disappearing below them.

They disembarked at the top for the next cable car which was waiting for them five hundred metres across the shoulder of the crest. This lift was also opened especially for them and a curt greeting passed between the lift operator and Berlini. Twenty minutes later they were at the top. A dim light was already burning in the bar-restaurant which served skiers. Berlini led the way into the cold room where a surly, sleep-befuddled Italian was brewing chocolate. They downed the hot drinks and hurried outside as twilight stole behind the dark mass of the Glocker. They fitted their skins, Berlini striding off and leading the way with Kim in the middle as the first hint of dawn flushed the slopes ahead of them. They were at 2300 metres and the Chamois hut was on the other side of the crest, over a thousand metres above them.

Dirk had never experienced cold of this intensity. His hands were numb and he worked his fingers inside his mitts; the going became harder, the air freezing about his lips as, panting, he inhaled more deeply through his mouth. Berlini was selecting long traverses across the slopes, climbing all the time, choosing the line that could gain the maximum of height with the minimum of effort.

Dirk followed carefully in Kim's tracks. She was going well, her slight figure swinging naturally into the rhythm of the climb. For the first hour, he had no difficulty in keeping up, but, as the height increased, the exertion began to tell. Breathing became more and more difficult, until he had to stop. He called out and Kim turned to wait for him.

He leaned on his sticks, trying to regain his breath. The air was so rarefied that the first gulps benefited him little, but after a few minutes he was again himself. At 8·35, the sun showed from behind the cloud sweeping across the tops. He waved and they set off again, step after step, towards the glacier that lay between them and the pass beginning to be distinguishable between the jumble of mountain tops. There must be nearly four hundred metres more to climb. For the first time, he wondered whether he would make it: his breathing was becoming more difficult with each stride that he took.

'Stop, Kim,' he gasped. He could go on no longer. '*STOP. . . .*' His heart was hammering against his ribs. The icy air which he drew down to the depths of his lungs scalded his throat.

'Don't shout,' Kim called, glancing upwards towards the blanket of snow mantling the slopes above them. She slithered down to help him. 'Berlini has avalanches on his mind and he's worried about the next traverse. Once we reach the glacier we'll be all right. Here, give me one of the packs.'

Before he knew what she was doing, she had prised the smaller haversack from him, the pack holding their clothes. 'Take it steadily,' she encouraged. 'Don't worry about Emmanuel. He won't leave us.'

'Give that back . . .'

'Go on ahead and I'll follow. Your body needs a lot more energy than mine to climb this gradient.'

She refused to budge until he had moved past her. Then he was off again, eyes glued to the tracks ahead of him, as he struggled after their guide. Berlini was waiting, but he did not conceal his impatience and contempt. Then he turned his back. Apathetically Dirk watched those piston legs pounding up the interminable slope. The guide gradually drew away, with Dirk trying to emulate the long strides. He began counting to decide how many paces he could manage before being forced to stop again for breath. This was shameful: a hulking ex-marine incapacitated by lack of oxygen – and a woman helping him to the top, carrying his load.

Thirty-five, thirty-six . . . breath . . . thirty-seven . . . he might make forty, but this white world was beginning to swim before his eyes . . . thirty-nine, forty. He slumped forwards to lean on his sticks. He was gasping for oxygen; he could not go on. His heart raced beneath his rib cage. Kim's skis hissed as she closed up behind him. Berlini had stopped also and was turning back to help his disappointing client.

'Sorry.' He gasped the apology as soon as he could draw breath. 'I must stop. Can't breathe . . .'

Kim and the guide had retreated a few yards and were talking together earnestly. Berlini swung his stick towards the glacier and glanced at his watch – 10·15 already. Kim slid back to him, her face serious.

'If we don't reach the glacier by a quarter to eleven, he'll turn back. He could have us down again in Limouro before we lose the light.'

'How far to go?' he gasped as he clawed for air. However much they bullied, his heart could not pump sufficient oxygen fast enough. His limbs were in spasm and were refusing to work.

'A few hundred yards, that's all.'

She was leaning on her sticks, peering up at him with fear in her eyes. She too was struggling for breath, but she seemed fit enough to go on.

'Okay. I'll get there on time, but be patient. . . . I've lived at sea level most of my life.'

He started again, his legs forcing the skis to follow in Berlini's tracks. The guide had decreased the gradient of climb and, though Dirk would have further to traverse, he might at least reach the top, if he could hold on for these last few hundred feet. Three more traverses should do it. . . . He turned and slowly climbed after the guide who, pausing frequently and turning round with frustration, was

59

pitilessly driving upwards towards the shoulder, where the glacier began.

Dirk never knew how he reached the top . . . He must have passed out, because Kim was bending over him, a cup in her hands, as Berlini held him upright. The world was swimming around him, the far peaks spiralling before his eyes. He felt the air entering his lungs again, then the pain diminished and his eyes began to focus. He was beyond caring now. They could leave him here, for God's sake. He would find his own way back . . .

He tasted the sweet lemonade trickling down his gullet. His mind cleared and he saw the suspicion of a smile on Berlini's face. 'It's 10·40,' Kim was saying. 'We're over the worst of the climb, Dirk.'

Normality was fast returning. 'What's he got for us now, Kim?'

'Just the glacier, than a small climb up to the pass. It's all downhill then until we reach the chalet. Emmanuel wants to know if you can go on. The mist is clamping down.'

'Tell him to give me a minute . . .'

He could see Berlini, ahead of him . . . derision, contempt or amusement at the futility of his client? Dirk heard the sound of steel on solid ice as the guide prodded the ground ahead of him.

'It's sheet ice,' Berlini said in his broken English. 'Don't fall here. Crevasses.' He uncurled the rope from about his shoulders. He turned and spoke to Dirk. 'Please. Signor come next to me.'

They roped up, Dirk following Berlini, Kim number three. The guide led off, feeling his first few steps across the ice. They had retained their skins to give more adhesion, but Dirk felt the first twinge of panic as his edges slithered across the slippery surface. He glanced downwards to the yawning crevasse, eighty metres below, just visible in the swirling mist.

'Follow,' Berlini called over his shoulder. He had extracted his alpenstock and, as Dirk inched on to the ice, he carefully took in the slack of the rope. Dirk felt the tug when Kim followed after him.

There must have been a ten-metre span between them. Each time, as Dirk reached Berlini, they half-turned to watch Kim. The glacier traverse was about a quarter of a mile long and seemed unending to Dirk. A false move and he would be down, slithering towards that dark abyss. How Berlini hoped to hold them, if either of his clients fell, was beyond Dirk's comprehension. He was as frightened as he had seldom been in his life: the cliff-scaling as a Royal Marine in Cornwall was nothing to this. The break in the shoulder was visible: there were only a few hundred metres to go.

'Careful, signor . . .'

The guide had reached the edge of the moraine. He turned again to watch his charges, when Dirk began his final effort to reach the patch of grit. As he thrust on his sticks, his skis slid from under him.

He came down hard on his left wrist. The ice slithered beneath his skis which were tangling beneath him, as he shot into the gradient of the glacier. As his hands clawed for any projection to halt his slide, he felt the jolt on the rope when Kim was jerked off balance. The white world began gyrating about him and he yelled in terror as the crevasse swirled towards him.

Chapter 10

Emmanuel Berlini felt sick with frustration as he saw the Englishman fall. He had so nearly negotiated this incompetent couple across the most dangerous section of the route – and, within metres of safety, the fool had slipped. With the instinct of a lifetime in the mountains he reacted to absorb the sudden, sickening wrench that could sweep them all to disaster. Kicking at the frozen ground, he straightened his knees and flung himself backwards, the heels of his boots jabbing into the iron-hard moraine. He had just time to take in the slack on the rope as the woman tumbled, flicked off balance by her companion's fall.

The couple swung in a parabola across the glistening ice. First, the man sprawling head-first downwards, legs and skis flailing. Then the girl, a bundle of red and blue, plummeting towards that gaping chasm. All depended on Berlini being able to absorb the shock. He braced every muscle in his body and waited for the jolt.

His arms were nearly wrenched from their sockets . . . either he was becoming old or the Englishman was heavier than Emmanuel had guessed. He cursed to himself. He should never have brought them – he had made a fundamental error, putting cash before judgment; after Rossi's recommendation, he had never suspected that the man could be so inept as this. The danger from avalanches was serious enough, let alone . . . and then the girl was screaming below.

For what seemed an eternity, they dangled there, on twenty metres of rope. Two lives suspended in his hands. He sighed with relief, but he still had to haul them up. He could see the girl's face was grey with terror as she hung across the lip of that bottomless crevasse. Carefully and deliberately he yanked a bight of the rope around the outcrop of rock at his back. A couple of turns – then they were safe.

It took him over half an hour to haul up both of them – thirty minutes of back-breaking work at this altitude. One mistake and the two English would slide back into the crevasse – but at least *he* was safe now. . . . Crouching down he hauled on the bight, heaving upwards, taking in the slack around the rock, gaining half a metre at each tug. Finally the Englishman scrambled shakily to his feet, and seconds later was joining him in the haul. A few heaves and the girl was safe, gasping and shocked, as she lay on the grit of the moraine.

'We lose time,' Berlini said, as the Englishman tried to express his thanks. 'We must move quick. Cloud no good.' He shook his head, began coiling up his rope and collecting his skis. 'Follow.'

He did not wait for them. They could hurry or be left to find their own way to the hut – this pair lacked any sense of urgency. It was past noon already, and if he made a mistake now, he could miss the Chamois hut. With this lowering cloud, it would be dark by four. He stomped across the moraine and heard his two clients scrabbling behind him. He reached the snow and snapped on his skis.

'Keep close,' he ordered. 'Signor first, then signora. . . .' He shortened the rope between them, checked the strands for chafe . . . there was no time to stop for food.

For the first time in months, Emmanuel Berlini felt anxiety gnawing at him. Next Sunday, he had that party of four to bring across. They had paid double price when he had hesitated; money had meant nothing to the big Iraqi. 'Get us across – and quick.' This had been the sum total of conversation. They had to reach Walther Kretchma's farm, like the others.

Emmanuel had learned never to ask questions in this game. He was a guide, no more, no less. What the parties carried, or whatever their destination, was no concern of his. . . . But Walther had done well by renting the farm this year. For over a year those geologists and scientists had been carrying out their researches from Kretchma's farm. They were a well-organized lot but did not give much away: some sort of government work apparently. Walther was uncommunicative now. Emmanuel no longer felt welcome there, even after a difficult crossing.

He halted at the cairn they had built last year. He had come unstuck here once: he could not afford a mistake today, with the cloud clamping down so thickly. If the visibility had not cleared by tomorrow, he doubted whether he'd be able to return to Limouro on the morrow. He cursed again, frustrated by this unnecessarily trying and pointless trip. Next Sunday's job was an important one for him.

'It's a two-hour run down to the Chamois,' he said. 'Keep close. We'll have to chance the avalanches.' His knowledge of the English language had stood him in good stead, with the number of Americans and Anglo-Saxons he was ferrying across.

Provided he could identify the rocks just ahead, he would make the hut all right. He was worried by these deteriorating conditions: if it blew hard tonight, the snow would be very unstable tomorrow – he wouldn't worry these idiots with that danger. He could always . . .

He felt uneasy, his instinct of self-preservation suddenly alerted. Where was that lichen-covered rock beneath the overhang of the outcrop? The first snowflakes were loitering down; visibility was almost zero, hardly safe enough for him, let alone for the weaker of his two charges. He must be getting old to feel so anxious – but nothing had gone right this trip. One of them needed only to fall badly, and he would be in real trouble – only an hour and a half to go before the light failed and the cold began to set in. He forced on as fast as he dared, the rope behind him twitching as the girl tried to keep up.

'*Halt . . .*'

The wind was getting up and the snow was swirling about them, the flakes driving into their faces. He could just see the tips of his skis and for a brief moment, he hated this savage environment, an emotion he did not often experience.

This spot was always difficult. The junction of the four gullies from this plateau at their heads, left too many options – he required the third lead. If he made a mistake, they would have a hard climb back – and the Englishman could not take much more.

He swore again. He would have to be certain before he led off. '*Wait here,*' he shouted against the wind.

He took the girl's elbow and pushed her into the lee of the outcrop. '*Don't move.*'

He left them and made the circuit of the plateau. He identified the gully entries by physically feeling the rock at the head of each. He had placed a pile of stones here in the summer to mark the route, but with this winter's heavy snowfall, he would never find it.

Identification was a matter of elimination – the Schreck lead was the third opening from his starting point. If he could not be sure, it might be safer to try to stick the night out – at least they could always find a lee here. Those who had survived a night up here, had always bivouacked. Only violent public outcry had produced the funds for the building of the Chamois hut.

Was that his personal cairn right ahead? He swept away the snow with his stick. Thank God. No doubts now. He planted his ski-stick hard into the snow and groped his way back for his charges. He would have to set as fast a pace as he dared if the Englishman was to reach the hut before dark . . . but from what he had seen, Trevallack on his *langlauf* skis, would be falling continually during the descent.

'Come . . .'

Two spectres loomed up out of the white curtain. He put the man first, right behind him, and told the girl to ski close to her companion's tracks. He slid to the head of the gully and retrieved his ski-stick. Once again, checking his bearing, once more, certain of his cairn, he pushed off into the greyness.

His goggles were useless. The cold and the swirling flakes stung his eyes, but, inclining his head for the whole descent, with one eye he could just distinguish the route ahead. The landmarks came up, one after the other, rocks and outcrops he recognized. A patch of lichen here, the shape of a cornice, the proportions of a gully – all were fitting into place. He felt a vast relief: barring accidents, he could not fail to find the Chamois hut. He increased the pressure, stretching Trevallack to his utmost. Now that the fellow could breathe, and although his glasses were giving him trouble, he was doing much better. The hiss of their skis behind him was music to his ears.

There it was – the hut. The Chamois – God, was he glad to see it . . . a hump of snow in the fast disappearing light. They had done well to make it so fast in these conditions. He swung his stick to the right and led off to the snowed-up chalet.

He had not realized, with the wind at their backs, that it was blowing so hard. They set to to clear away the piled up snow. He and Trevallack heaved with their backs against the door, then fell heavily inside, when it suddenly opened. Laughing, the Englishman picked himself up. He was extending his hand in comradeship, but Berlini was concerned only with warming up their bodies before they froze to death.

'Signor, fetch some wood from the corner. Get the fire going, while I help the signora with the cooking stove.'

They piled their skis and sticks into the racks at the end of the hut and set about lighting the fire. The back-breaking work of lugging up the wood in the tractors during the summer would be justified tonight. He watched the flicker of flame from the central stove and knew that they were safe. He smiled at the girl, then lit the first of the two hurricane lanterns.

'The food's in the cupboard in the corner. There's soup and chocolate, and there's a choice of tins of ham or sausage and plenty of sauerkraut.'

The couple were livening up and talking. One thing about them, they had guts, even if they were lousy skiers. He sat at the table watching the girl hotting up the dehydrated soup flakes. She was a competent woman, too self-contained, but not bad looking. Her colouring and red hair reminded him of his cousin who came from the Valle d'Aosta. The heavily built Englishman was raising his cup of chocolate in salutation.

'Here's to our guide . . . cheers.'

'Thanks, Emmanuel,' the girl added, as she joined them with her mug of soup. The stuff tasted good and soon they were asking for more. They kept her at it, but were smiling now, though they had to shout against the howling wind outside.

'It'll be a bad night,' Berlini said. 'The hut's well built. We all shared in the work last summer. We brought the timber from Italy. The Austrians provided the accessories – and the beer, but that's all gone.'

They demolished the sausage and the ham, then finished off with the sauerkraut which he insisted on cooking himself. They thawed snow for water – not for a long time had a meal gone down so well. Kim tracked down a tin of coffee while Berlini lit his first pipe of the day. Around the fire roaring from the draught provided by the gale, they yarned away the time until drowsiness set in.

'You were worried this morning, Emmanuel,' Trevallack said, forcing a smile. 'Was I as bad as all that?'

'You were holding us up. I had no time in hand should we run into difficulties . . . and the snow conditions bothered me.' He was succeeding with his English and they understood him as he explained the rudiments of snow craft.

'You have to know your snow conditions. The north slopes are dangerous now. It's been a very cold winter and the surface is hard. You have to recognize the avalanche danger [he spoke the old Italian word, *lavina*, from his childhood days, but he used *lawine* when talking to the Austrians]. If you don't take the trouble to read your snow, the avalanche will get you sooner or later. It's difficult enough, if you've lived all your life in the mountains.'

He paused, sucking his pipe as he gazed into the flickering flames. The warmth and the fire were mesmerizing him and he was content to talk while the two strangers listened in silence. It was as well that they were absorbing his words, because, if the wind dropped in the night and tomorrow was fine . . . he couldn't risk being late for Sunday. It was simple enough to Schreck and was only seven kilometres down the Stromf valley.

'I've only heard avalanches, down in the valleys,' Trevallack said. 'They sound frightening enough. Tell us about them.'

'It'll take a long time.'

He talked softly, explaining the causes of the White Death, as the avalanche was known, throughout the Alps. Unstable snow conditions, the temperature effect, the orientation of the slope, the gradients – how they all played their part. The worst of the avalanches, the airborne powder monsters; and the wet and dry avalanches; how the hurricane-force winds produced destructive pressures of one kilogram per square centimetre – a large avalanche, crashing down from a two-thousand-metre drop, would be travelling at speeds of over 330 kilometres per hour and be producing destructive pressures 1571 times as powerful as a hurricane.

'What chance does a man stand if he's caught in an avalanche?'

'About one in three of being dug out alive. Death from an avalanche isn't a pretty sight.' He wanted to change the subject – he'd seen too many corpses twisted in the snow. Sometimes death occurred immediately from the terrible injuries received from the rocks beneath – a more merciful end than death by slow suffocation and drowning in the snow or in one's own vomit. The blue and purple faces, the crushed bodies, the twisted and contorted wrecks that so little time before had been normal, carefree, skiing human beings.

'God forbid you ever get caught in one,' he said. Then came the inevitable question, but from the woman this time:

'What's the best thing to do? If you're overwhelmed?'

'If you have time, slip the straps of your sticks from your wrists; free your bindings and try with all your might to swim up to the surface. You can be killed in only a metre of snow. Better never to get caught in one. Stay at home, but even that's not safe if *lavina* decides to attack a village. Houses are sliced in two, railway locomotives weighing over 120 tonnes are snatched from the rails like toys. The blast effect hurtling ahead of an airborne powder *lavina* seems to generate its own whirlwind effect.' He went on to tell them of the man he knew who had been picked up like a leaf and hurled about a kilometre through a vertical height of over 750 metres. Though injured, the man had, incredibly, survived. Berlini had seen the results of airborne powder avalanches – even the concrete had been blown out from between the reinforcing wires of a thirty-centimetre concrete wall.

An airborne powder avalanche could travel ten or eleven kilometres, turn through right-angle corners, bounce off opposing slopes, but still retain sufficient energy to annihilate houses and to lay waste acres of pine forest.

They were silent when finally they crawled into the pinewood bunks. Berlini was taking a long time to fall asleep. The snow was driving hard and the wind must be gale force as it battered against the buried hut. The howling crescendos and the sudden gusts were unnerving even him. Trevallack was to see to the first tending of the fire during the night – they would soon know if the fire went out. Emmanuel had had enough. He did not relish what he had to do in the morning, if it broke fine and clear. He turned over again and fell into a fitful sleep.

Chapter 11

She was awoken by the smell of the chocolate that Emmanuel was brewing. It was still dark, but the hut was strangely silent after the tumult of the night. The reflections of the flames from the wood that was crackling in the stove flickered across the roof beams. She needed urgently to use the rudimentary loo in the far corner – the cold had kept them all busy during the night – and she slipped out from the bunk whilst their guide was busied with getting breakfast.

She splashed about her face some melted snow from the bucket, felt the astringent tautness of the cold. The splitting headache of the night was almost gone. She crossed to Dirk's bunk and shook his shoulder.

'Time you got up. The guide's getting ready.'

She gazed down upon the shapeless form curled into the thick blankets. During the night, only his snores betrayed that he was alive. He was in need of a shave, but in repose, the lines were relaxed. He had lost that hard expression she had disliked so intensely in Beirut. She bent over him and touched his forehead with her lips.

'What time is it?' Suddenly he was awake and staring up at her, a faint smile twitching at the corners of his mouth.

'Nearly 5.30. Berlini's getting breakfast.'

She threw her anorak over the sweater she had worn all night. She ran a comb through her hair; there was not a minute to be lost if they were to reach Schreck before mid-afternoon. Three hours at the most, the guide had said.

They were ready by six, the hut cleaned up after their breakfast of hot chocolate and the muesli which Emmanuel had found in a metal bin. She felt the urge to go on, the thrill of a new day in these mountains suddenly heightened her awareness in everything around her. Her nerves tingled as Berlini heaved open the door of the hut. A heap of snow cascaded through the opening. It was still dark outside and the blast of cold air made her catch her breath.

There was not a breath of wind. The morning stars shivered in the bowl of the night sky. As she looked, it was so beautiful that she wished the moment could last, never to pass. Life was good, after the terrors of yesterday.

They went back into the hut and huddled round the failing embers while waiting for daylight. The guide seemed preoccupied with his own thoughts and nothing that Dirk could say could draw Berlini from his shell. At 6.45 the guide glanced again at his wrist watch, grunted and collected his sticks and skis. He waited for them, then closed the door behind them when they gathered outside. The greyness of dawn was stealing across the fresh snow, over a metre of it, which had driven against the hut during the night. By the time they had checked the shutters and battened up the door, the rose flush of dawn was kissing the peaks and stealing down the flanks of the mountains.

Berlini waited for them at the top of the rise leading towards the run down to the Schreckhorn valley. To their left was the route across the frontier from which they had come. It did not appear as steep as it had seemed when they had skied down in the failing light yesterday. The wind had built up great drifts of snow and it was impossible to identify their route.

'That's the Schreck valley,' Berlini said, pointing to a gap through the terrain a thousand metres below them. 'You take that ridge and then the long traverse until you reach the Walther farm, one of the highest in the valley, three hundred metres above Schreck. The chalet is well sheltered and you can't miss it. Can you see that cornice, just to the left of those two outcrops? See them?'

He was identifying the run down, a drop of a thousand metres, and easy all the way. With careful going, the trip would not take more than three hours. 'Watch out for avalanche conditions,' he said. 'The snow might be unstable today, after last night's wind. This is a north-facing slope.'

She was at a loss to understand his precise instructions. He had led with authority yesterday and they had done their best to follow conscientiously. He was in bad humour this morning, morose and itching to be off. She had never cared for him – an unusually arrogant man for one of these mountain people.

'Signor,' Berlini said sharply, his eyes meeting Dirk's momentarily. 'You promised you'd pay me in Austrian schillings.'

'Right,' Dirk replied brusquely. 'What of it?'

'Before we start, I'd like to see them.'

Dirk seemed taken aback. He was at a loss for words, but as he drew off his mitts to feel for the sock tied around his waist, Kim could sense his anger as he extracted the notes for Berlini to see. 'There you are, Berlini, in case you doubt my word. Marks, dollars, the lot. I'll change it when we reach Schreck.'

The Italian was dissatisfied. 'Show me the dollars, signor. How many do you owe me for the balance?'

'You can have it in schillings when we reach a bank in Schreck. *Here*, . . .' and he began counting out the green-backed bills.

Kim had turned her back on the embarrassing scene. She heard a cry, then '. . . *you bastard*,' from Dirk. 'Give them back.'

She turned to see Berlini, a fistful of banknotes in his right hand, driving powerfully away from them on his skis. His sticks and arms were flailing like pistons and already he was on the route back to Italy.

'Come back, you . . .' Dirk flushed with rage. He turned to her, incredulity on his face. 'Can you believe it? He's left us to find our own way down.'

She felt Dirk's frustration and she hurried after him as, in a frenzy of useless rage, he scrabbled after the guide. Dirk halted on the crest overlooking the frontier.

They felt the sun's first warmth as they stood there, utterly alone, shocked by the enormity of Berlini's callousness. 'I could murder him, Kim. What idiots he took us for. He meant to have us, I'm certain, since last night.'

The sun was lighting up the whole range, the Italian valleys blue, where they lingered in the lee of their ranges for the warmth that shortly would be bringing an end to this long, cold winter. A low rumble echoed up from one of the valleys to the eastwards and seconds later Kim spotted a white cloud drifting across the lower slopes.

'One of his famous avalanches,' Dirk said. 'I almost hope he gets caught in one.'

She took his arm and led him back to their starting point for their run down. 'Come on,' she said. 'Take the lead and I'll follow.'

They slung their gear across their backs, hopefully for the last time. There were no customs problems now. They were in Austria and within twelve kilometres of Schreck. It would be good to be shot of the codes and to enjoy a comfortable night. They had only to wait for the bank's president to arrive and then life could return to normality.

As she followed in Dirk's tracks, she tried to force behind her the thoughts that were now too often stealing into her mind. The faults she had previously seen in him, were now, she realized, some of his qualities – that bluff exterior concealed a gentleness she had not known existed: his arrogance reflected only the pride he had felt for the Service in which he had been a part. Loyalty was no crime – a refreshing surprise today, when cynicism was god. She watched him swinging down the slope, confident in himself again.

God, it was marvellous to feel alive after these years of remorse and self-pity. Who knew what the future might bring? She could leave the slow death of loneliness behind her now, if things could only develop naturally. Her heart had thawed but she must guard it well. She had a horror of appearing ridiculous in his eyes.

'C'mon, Kim . . .'

He was waiting for her by the cornice, that white cliff of over-hanging snow. There was no other track down – and even with her limited experience, she knew that it was dangerous here. The snow was hard-packed from the cold and the strong winds of overnight. Even a shout or a shot reverberating through a valley could trigger off an avalanche, they said, but Berlini had treated the belief with scorn. She slithered up to Dirk and they stood together for a moment to sight the route ahead.

'Too fast for you?' he asked. 'Would you like to lead?'

'Too slow,' she laughed. 'Let's stop a moment. It's glorious here and we've got all day.'

'Provided the weather holds. God knows what we'll do if it clamps down like yesterday.'

They paused there briefly, on the crest beneath the burgeoned cornice. Ahead stretched a vast snowfield, an exhilarating traverse across to the cleft in the saddle which the guide had identified. Twenty metres beneath them, a rounded shoulder was concealing a small gully running out to the right.

'Not happy,' she said.

'Why?'

'From what Berlini said, this snow could be unstable.'

'Meaning?'

'From what I've learned through the years and from what that bastard said last night, we've had a lot of snow. It's been unusually cold for weeks and the wind has hardened the crust. It's too warm this morning. This lot could slide.'

He said nothing, screwing up his eyes from the glare. He pulled down his goggles over his glasses, then deliberately unstrapped the sticks from his wrists. He turned and leaned against her.

'Mebbe you're right. You'd better do the same.'

She slipped her wrists from the straps. She sensed for a moment, as he leaned against her, that he was about to kiss her. She did not move, watching him, when he stiffened suddenly and twisted away from her. There was a flurry of snow beneath them and then she saw the black shaft of his ski stick slipping down the slope. It reached the shoulder of the gully, toppled over the edge and disappeared.

They did not speak. Dirk was skiing just within his limits and with only one stick, he would have a job getting down. If the weather soured and they lost the light . . .

'Hold my haversack,' she said. 'Won't take a minute.'

Before he could protest, she was negotiating the ledge and turning to halt on the crest above the gully. She peered over the edge. At the bottom of a flurry in the snow, his stick was plainly visible. She could climb down the steep bit, then turn to reach the spot where the stick rested.

The gradient here was steep and she took it carefully. She pointed to the stick and turned to wave briefly at Dirk. His thick figure stood black against the white cornice behind him but, after a few steps, he was lost to sight. She rested a moment, his stick only fifty metres below her. The going would be safer if she walked down, so, discarding her skis, she tossed them and one stick over the lip at the side of the gully. Gingerly she stepped down, taking her weight on her left stick as she descended upon the hard surface of the crusted snow. She was suddenly frightened . . . if she broke an ankle here. . .? She stopped again and saw her skis against the sky-line, a few metres away.

What happened next remained in her memory for the rest of her life. The snow quivered beneath her. There was a dull explosion, then a violent underground shock. In horror, she watched rifts opening around her, then streaking across the snow. She turned and saw a mound of snow pouncing down upon her like a tidal wave.

She fell, overwhelmed by the enveloping mass. She knew that she had been within a metre of the edge of the left-hand side of the gully, so she kicked frenziedly towards where the lip might be. Snow was filling her nostrils and smothering her face. She remembered what Berlini had told them . . . cover the head to preserve breathing space; shield the face in the crook of the arm; swim with utmost strength towards the surface. She was choking and fighting for breath when she felt a violent pain stabbing in her back. For an instant she glimpsed light above her. Then she was buried again, rolled over and over, her world dark, suffocating, terrible. She recognized death and felt the terror. If she could only survive this first onslaught, she might have a chance – turn and fight, dig an air trap. She heard her muffled screaming and knew that her efforts were pointless. She was pinioned in this sea of pulverizing snow. Who could possibly hear her now . . . ?

A terrible weight was crushing her body, clamping her rib-cage so that she could not exhale. As her world went black about her, she felt the speed of the avalanche diminishing. A sudden brightness broke over her and, as she came to a halt, the snow above her seemed lighter, finer, like a corpse's shroud. Hysterically, she scrambled towards that feeble glimmer, groping for the life-giving air so tantalizingly near. . . . She scrabbled with her fingers, staining the snow with her blood as she flailed desperately with her arms and elbows to escape the suffocating embrace.

Suddenly, there was air. She sucked in the stuff to the depths of her lungs. No longer that choking white death. . . . The fingers of her right hand clawed through the surface; the sunlight flickered above her as she scooped a trough above her head. She realized then that she could not move . . .

Slowly, sanity returned. If she could see the daylight she *must* be on the edge of the gully. Dirk would find her quickly . . . then, with horror, she remembered that he had been standing beneath the cornice.

The avalanche which she had released could have dislodged the blanket of snow overhanging the ledge on which he had been standing. She might have triggered off the whole mass above them – God, what an end to a beginning. . . . She tried to fight the panic. *Keep your cool, girl. You can get out of this . . .*

Chapter 12

What a bloody idiot he had been to lose his stick – even though Kim was quicker on her skis than he was, they would lose time retrieving the thing. He glanced impatiently at his watch as she appeared again below the shoulder: 8.57. Plenty of time in hand . . .

She had halted at the top and was indicating the position of his stick as she waved to him. She was taking off her skis and tossing them across to the left-hand edge of the gully. She seemed to hesitate and was prodding at the packed snow before she began her descent.

The puff of white, powdery smoke was not immediately significant. He heard a muffled explosion, then saw the cracks streaking across the surface of the hard-packed snow. The gully seemed to heave and then the white mass began to slide, slowly at first, then with terrifying speed.

He bellowed his warning but there was nothing she could do. She turned, horror frozen on her face, as she watched the avalanche overwhelming her. The snow, on which she had been standing a second before, broke away above her and began to roll over her, like one of those gigantic breakers on his north Cornish coast . . .

Suddenly there was a roaring about his ears as the shock of tons of snow smothered him. Instinctively he kicked out, hurling himself backwards, away from the cornice. His head struck hard on the snow and then he could not move, his legs trapped by the skis which were pinioned by the weight of the snow. He released his grip from his remaining stick and buried his head in his arms, trying with his elbows to jostle space for a pocket of air.

Panic kills. Panic, just as at sea. You're drowning, Trevallack, up in these bloody mountains. Kim's avalanche must have released the snow above the cornice. He could hear nothing now but the gasping of his own breathing. It was dark here, black as pitch . . . and down there Kim was dying, trapped too by this White Death as Berlini called it. *God, finish it quickly. This suffocating agony. . . . I can't move a bloody thing . . . they'll find the codes in the spring thaw when they find my putrefying body. . . .* His lungs were on fire, his heart hammering again, like yesterday. He scrabbled frenziedly to enlarge the hole about him. But as he racked his lungs, trying to exhale against the weight that was crushing him, the snow filled his nostrils, choked his mouth and gullet. . . . Faintly he heard the gurgling in his throat as his breathing became more feeble. His thoughts became confused as his brain refused to reason. His mind began to wheel, spinning, faster, faster. . . . His stomach heaved in spasms as he vomited in the terror of the darkness . . .

It was the basket of his stick that she saw first – a black pinprick in the jumble of snow. She was still panting for breath, after her frenzied scramble up the forty yards back to the cornice. Mercifully, her hand had clenched round her stick in the darkness: it was only because she still had it with her that she had reached the top again so quickly. She scrabbled with her mitts at the snow, following down the shaft of his stick. He *was* there, his hand cold – and then his arm. She was calling his name, moaning with terror and shock. She forced herself to look when she uncovered the body.

He had lost consciousness, but was still breathing. His face had that florid blue tinge that betokened death from suffocation. *God, oh God, don't let him die – no, no, please* . . . and she straddled him with her own body to give him warmth. Free the nose, clear the vomit – she forced back his chin, pulled out his tongue, creased her fingers about his nose, clamped her mouth to his. Then, deeply, rhythmically, drawing in great gobs of air, she breathed her life-giving oxygen back into his lungs.

She never knew how long she gave him resuscitation. There was no response at first, merely her own exhalations. She stuffed her hand beneath his shirt, but could feel no pulse. Continue, they'd told her, even after you think it's a cadaver – there was always a chance. She felt no revulsion as she had done on the dummies in the first aid classes; then she sensed it, the faint but regular beat of his heart as it picked up again the rhythmical pumping that brought back life. She was beginning to feel dizzy, sweating from the exertion in the sun. She could not keep it up much longer or she'd pass out herself. . . . His eyelids were flickering. His eyes rolled back in their sockets, then swivelled slowly, searching for her, trying to focus on her face.

'Speak, for God's sake . . .'

She tried to haul him to a sitting position, with the snow at his back, but he was barely conscious and moaning to himself. As he regained his senses he stretched out his arms to her.

She encircled him with her arms, the tears streaming down her face. They sat together, basking in the forenoon sun while the warmth slowly brought them to reality. She lost count of time. The world was bright about them, the sky, a brilliant blue and they were alive.

He saw those green-flecked eyes, like a cat's, close to him. Then they faded away, like a zoom lens, but blurred and out of focus.

'It's like coming back from the dead.' He gripped her hand, terrified she would melt away again.

'It's you, Kim?'

'It's me. . . .' He felt the warmth of her body. He watched the tears coursing down her cheeks as she cleaned him up. Then she took his hand and stroked the back of his wrist.

'I've damaged my leg – above the ankle,' he said.

He fumbled with the left buckle of his breeches, but his movements were unco-ordinated and feeble. She helped him, rolling down the wet stocking. She saw the blood on her hands and inspected the wound across the back of his calf.

'It's a deep cut. A flap of skin needs stitching together.'

She found a handkerchief in the pocket of his anorak. She staunched the blood and firmly bound the wound. He was very cold. He was trembling spasmodically and he could not prevent his teeth chattering.

'Stand up, if you can. Get your circulation going.'

She dragged him to his feet and he stood there groggily, leaning on her shoulder while she propped him up. The mountains slowly ceased to spin around him; and the pain in his chest was lessening.

'What's the time?'

'10.45.' She was gently forcing his fingers round one of her skisticks. 'You'll need this. I'll never find yours now.'

They peered down at the gully which was now a confusion of snow.

'My God,' he said, speaking his thoughts aloud. 'It's not a hundred metres long – and less than forty wide.'

She urged him forwards towards the snowfield ahead of them.

'At its deepest, it's barely two metres,' she said. 'It's these little ones that trap the lone skiers. What must it be like when a mountainside hurtles down?'

'Let's get going, Kim. I've had enough of this.'

'Your colour's coming back. Okay to start?'

'You lead,' he said. 'We ought to be spaced well. If *that* could slide, this whole face must be unstable.'

They stared at each other. The vast white field ahead was waiting for them. Kim picked up her skis.

'I'll go first,' he continued briskly. 'I'm the heavier. If it's okay for me, you'll be all right in my tracks. Fifty metres, Berlini said.'

She continued to argue until he lost his patience. 'You stubborn woman,' he began, when suddenly she pointed with her stick.

'Look, Dirk, there's a mark ahead, across on the other side.' He screwed up his eyes – and there it was, a pole with a red circle across the top.

'A red run, Kim. It's a red run. . . .' He was shouting with excitement. 'We've reached civilization.' On an impulse, he encircled her with his arm, as a feeling of tenderness swept through him for this woman who had saved his life. She was peering up at him, a question in her eyes. They were both suffering from shock, but his words were a torrent as they poured from him. He ended lamely: 'You're a wonderful person, Kim. Not many women . . .' He felt her gentle resistance as she freed herself.

'Better get going,' she said. 'Wait for me when you reach the other side.'

He pushed off petulantly, across the hard surface that was the flank of this interminable mountain. He glided slowly across the white sheet, turning momentarily to be sure she was following. So far, so good – and he tried to sponge from his imagination the fate awaiting them if this slab broke away. There would be no chance, if this mountainside released . . .

The silent mountain was waiting to spring the trap . . . but there was only five hundred metres to that break in the shoulder and the red pole which marked the run down to Schreck. They would be in the tree line soon. This was bloody awful. Claustrophobia must be like this: mine shafts, submarines. . . . He felt the panic – they were so near – then he had reached the marker and the cleft in the ridge. He could not control the trembling. . . . He had never experienced such terror in his life . . . and then she was by his side.

'Look, Dirk . . .'

She had over-run him through the cleft in the snow-covered rocks and was gazing down the other side of the cleft.

Five hundred metres below, a pine wood stretched across the mountainside. On the far side of the trees, a spiral of blue smoke curled into the air.

He knew that she was crying, but she was ashamed of her tears. He left her alone, then followed as she led off to the track through the trees, going well, though skiing with only one stick. She waited for him at the far side of the wood. Nestling into a snowy hillock was a farm house, sheltered and protected from avalanche hazard by the thickly wooded slope above it. They hurried on, impatient to start on their last stage to Schreck. They emerged from the wood, but were surprised to be halted by a warning notice on a ten-foot grille fence: *'Research Station – Entry Forbidden'*. They leaned on their sticks, dismayed by the unfriendliness of this brooding farmstead. The fence, Dirk reckoned, must be enclosing an acre of land. In the background, a diesel generator was pounding rhythmically.

'C'mon. Let's see if there's anyone about.'

The sweet smell of a wood fire drifted up from the chimney at the end of the house. They reached first the rear of the cowshed which comprised half the farmstead. In the sunshine, a cow was munching contentedly, tethered in its minuscule yard. The friendly smell of ammonia wafted upwards in the still air; as a wisp of steam spiralled upwards from the peak of its conical dung heap. The walls of the exposed side of the house were grey with the rotting wooden slats shielding the dwelling from the wet. The other two sides were half-buried; on the windward side, an ancient grass cutter was propped against the wall; and the rusting body of an old Ford was serving as a henhouse for the clutch of hens pecking at the cleared patch in the snow.

They found the entrance on the southern side, where a barred gate kept out all visitors. The farm looked down upon a steep-sided valley which cradled the village of Schreck between its flanks. On the same side as Walther Kretchma's farm, a heavily wooded slope concealed most of the village. The onion-dome of the church was visible, as also were the cables of the telecabin linking Schreck with the crest of the Krabach Kopf. A pylon jutted up from the cliff-face, two-thirds up the mountain; the wires of the cable car were slung over the valley, obliquely across the afforested mountainside. Opposite, a modern hotel basked in the sun at the foot of the south-facing slopes rearing up behind it. A road snaked up from behind the wood, but there were no other dwellings in sight. Even from here, five hundred metres above the hotel, Dirk judged, he could see the translucent swimming pool steaming in its glass dome.

A dog was barking: they could hear its chain rasping against its kennel.

'You do the talking,' Kim said. 'Your German's better than mine.'

'Berlini was right. You don't get much of a welcome.'

He yanked at the bell on the gatepost and the huge dog went berserk. While they waited, they had time to absorb the geography of the research station.

On the windward side of the roof, a complex of meteorological instruments turned idly in the breeze that was getting up with mid-day. A steel lattice mast with a whip aerial had been built between the cattle yard and the main house. A duplicate erection stood on a small hillock at the far end of the property. A thick cable ran inside the lattice and its aerial, taller than the other, was heavily insulated. Off the old house and visible only from the side, was a newly-built concrete L-shaped wing. Its windows were shut and barred; two wide doors, also shut, seemed to be the only entrance.

A tall Austrian, in a black hat, old leather trousers and a green woollen smock, was peering at them from the corner of the yard. He was approaching truculently, wiping his hands on his haunches.

'*Ja?* What d'you want?'

Dirk's German had always been good and the man's attitude became less hostile.

'A bad cut, is it? The doctor's near the church, at the top of the village.'

'Nothing serious. Needs cleaning up a bit. Can you spare me a bandage?'

The man hesitated, his eyes darting over their shoulders.

He unlocked the gate and hurried them inside the compound. He locked the portals behind them and pushed Dirk inside the old building, curtly telling Kim to wait outside. He allowed Dirk into the curtained kitchen at the end of the smoky room. He pointed to the sink, while he produced a grubby bandage from a cupboard. 'Help yourself,' he grunted. 'Get a move on. I've much work this morning.' He pushed a bottle of schnapps across the sink. 'That'll keep it antiseptic until you reach the doctor.'

The alcohol stung but the Austrian offered no help, said nothing. His impatience at having to lose time on these feckless skiers was hardly concealed.

'Thanks.'

They returned to the brightness outside. Kim was strolling back from the direction of the hen run. Walther Kretchma rounded on her, swearing in guttural German. He unleashed the dog and held it, its teeth bared, its hackles stiff, snarling at their heels.

'Let's get out,' Dirk said. 'We're not welcome, are we, Herr Kretchma?'

The tall, gaunt man halted, his hands on the lock.

'How d'you know my name?'

'Emmanuel . . .'

'Berlini?'

'Yes. Friend of yours?'

Kretchma stiffened suddenly, as a bell began ringing from the corner of the new building. A band of skiers was approaching through the trees. Kretchma snapped open the lock and was pushing Kim through the gate when the first man in the party swished through the gap in the wood, a cascade of snow at his heels as he swept to a stop, a yard ahead of Kim. He shot a glance at Kretchma and, as the other two arrived behind him, the chatter ceased. The chirping of the sparrows and the whining of the Alsatian dog were the only sounds in the abrupt silence.

'What are you doing here?'

'The man's badly cut, Herr Sciacca. He asked for help.'

Ignoring the Austrian farmer, the leader of the party spoke softly, in perfect English. His black eyes, set widely apart in his Latin face, bore into Dirk. There was a reptilian repulsion about him which was inexplicable.

'I was hoping to find help – and a welcome,' Dirk snapped. 'Herr Kretchma has lent me a bandage, but he hasn't fallen over himself . . .'

'He has orders to refuse all entry into the research centre. Are you incapable of reading the notice? It's dangerous here, unless you know what you're doing.'

'We've had an accident.'

Their leader was an unpleasant bastard. He slid close to Dirk and shoved his face within a foot of the Englishman's. Dirk saw the fire flickering in those fanatical, restless eyes. The man was about forty and of the same height as Dirk, but twice as stocky. A mountain of a man, he was strong as a gorilla, with long arms, and hands as big as hams which were clenching the handles of his sticks.

Judging by the nervousness on the faces of his companions, they were afraid of their formidable leader.

'Your presence here is against regulations. *Here, Tobol.* . . .' He flicked his finger, Kretchma slipped the lead, and in one bound the Alsatian was cowering at his master's feet, its ruff was rigid as it bared its teeth, ready to spring at the strangers who had strayed in from the cold.

'Tobol is usually free-roaming,' Herr Sciacca said. 'I shouldn't trespass again, not if you want to avoid accidents.' He swung round to the man at his back, a tall, lean character, tough, with a fine physique. 'Zydek, see these people off the premises.'

Dirk jerked his arms free of the officious henchman who was about twenty-five, head and shoulders above the other skiers at the end of the line – a small, middle-aged character with an owlish look of innocence about his professional face.

'Leave her alone.'

In his anger, Dirk swung out with his stick and caught the man they called Zydek, a clout across the head. The man turned slowly, his face a study of amazed disbelief.

'*Get out of my way.*' Dirk shoved against the Austrian. The man toppled into the snow.

'*Clear out,*' Sciacca snapped.

Dirk shoved off, not bothering to turn round. Kim was safely ahead and was already skiing down the Schreck run. 'You've got one minute to quit this territory,' Sciacca was yelling.

Dirk pushed on, the snow hissing beneath his skis. Behind him he heard the baying of the gigantic hound.

Chapter 13

The descent to Schreck took longer than they expected. The lights in the windows were warm and welcoming, as Dirk glided down the final run-in at the top of the village. Kim had led the way down, but she had waited for him by the supermarket, the huge chalet servicing the little ski resort with its needs. They unsnapped their skis. With great relief, they joined the jostling skiers returning for the night.

'It all seems so unreal, Kim,' he said, blocking her way across the ice-hardened pavement running along the side of the River Schreck. 'I'd never have made it without you.'

She leaned against him, oblivious to the stream of humanity. She was stifling back the tears as she stood there, unable to face the mundane problems ahead of them. She seemed so small and shrunken, her skis crossed over her shoulder, her one stick in her hand. Her cheeks were drawn and she was at the end of her tether. He must find accommodation, for the cold of the evening was already beginning to bite.

'I'll take your skis.' He prised them from her and elbowed his way to the tourist bureau across the road.

The warmth of the office and the buzz of conversation brought them back to reality, as they waited their turn at the counter. They had only to deliver the codes and their duty was done. The girl on the other side of the desk was looking curiously at him.

'Rooms for the night? Sorry, sir. There's not a bed available in Schreck.'

The girl was impatient to shut the bureau for the night. She was trying to dismiss them, but the desperation on Dirk's face must have made her hesitate. She used her phone, then glanced up at them, smiling briefly.

'My uncle says he can help over the weekend,' she said. 'He's got one bed in the family house and one over the machinery room. You'll find something on Monday as there are often cancellations then.'

Dirk muttered his thanks in his best German.

'Family Strauss,' she said. 'You can't miss their chalet. It's the Krabach Kopf *seilbahn* and my uncle Rudi is the manager.'

They trudged up the village street, fighting against the icy wind sweeping down the valley. The bars were busy with their *gluweins* and hot chocolates, but all Dirk and Kim craved for was a roof for the night. Finally they identified the large, sloping roof of the cable-car station. In the gloom of the grey evening, the building stood aloof from the bright lights and tinsel of the remainder of Schreck.

'Herr Strauss? The tourist office sent us.'

Rudi Strauss was a small, thickset man with the taut face of a life used to discipline and responsibilities. His wife, Marthe, welcomed them inside. She fussed over Kim as if she had been her own daughter.

'Came across the top yesterday, did you?' Strauss asked, shaking his head. 'You must eat.' He asked no more questions, but took Dirk up two flights of stairs to a small room below the eaves of the roof. 'It's over the machinery room,' he explained. 'The first lift is not till seven in the morning. You won't be disturbed.'

Dirk dumped his gear on the camp bed.

'The toilet's downstairs,' Strauss added apologetically. 'You'll eat with us now? Supper's on the table.'

Kim was already seated at the table when they returned downstairs. A dark-haired girl, Anna, and her blond husband, Hans, were drawing her into the conversation while Frau Strauss ladled the soup.

'How long are you staying in Schreck, Herr Trevallack?' Strauss had learned his English when working with Dorman Long.

'Not long enough. I'm new to this part of the world.'

Strauss shook his grizzled head. 'Schreck is being spoilt, like all the rest. Since they built that new hotel, we've been swamped by strangers.'

'The Schreckhorn?'

'*Ja*. The promoters built it outside the village, as a rich man's retreat from the world. The clientéle doesn't ski much. It's mostly for international organizations and European conferences. There's an important one starting there this week.'

Strauss swallowed his beer and he seemed keen to talk to someone outside the family circle. He put Dirk next to him, as Kim and the rest of the family attacked the wholesome meal. The warmth, the beer, the calf's liver and the relaxed atmosphere drew Dirk from his lethargy. He took to Rudi Strauss and over the proffered black cigar, they yarned away the evening, Dirk with his passable German; Rudi, his excellent English.

'Why doesn't the Schreckhorn Hotel mix with the village?' Dirk asked. 'They need Schreck's services, surely?'

Strauss rubbed the stubble on his chin. The coffee was circulating and the end of the long day was beginning to tell. 'They started badly,' he said. 'Seven years ago, when they submitted their plans to build the hotel, the council and the mayor were strongly opposed to an external venture being allowed to steam-roller the traditions of the village. The capital comes from Vienna and the company runs a national chain of hotels.'

'How did it get built, then?'

'We objected to a building in the village, but when the promoters applied to build up the valley, on Strolz's farm, there was little we could do to stop it.' Then Strauss added with a wry grin: 'The old 'uns in the village didn't mind too much: the valley has an evil reputation. We don't go there unless we have to.'

Dirk accepted the schnapps and waited for Strauss to continue.

'It's cursed, they say. Goes back a long time.' He seemed reluctant to go on. He was shaking his head and seemed to be talking to himself. 'We should never have let them build. They'll swindle us, as the city people always do. Once the building has gone up, what can we do?'

'I've only seen it at a distance,' Dirk said. 'Modern chalet type, isn't it? Doesn't seem too bad, but I can't understand why it's on its own.'

'Superstition. They say there was a catastrophic avalanche in the valley centuries ago – the hospice archives record a disaster in the sixteen hundreds. The superstition has persisted ever since – and, anyway, the hotel took the risk upon themselves. We have never taken any notice of the danger, except that we will almost certainly have to help pay for the defences. *That* is the cause of the bad feeling.'

They had pushed back the supper things and drawn their chairs around the log fire that was spluttering in the stone-flagged chimney piece. The reflection of the flames flickered across the ceiling beams and upon the leathery face staring into the fire.

'What defences?' Dirk asked softly.

'Against the *lawine*. We never liked old Strolz and he, like all of us, treated the curse as an old wives' tale. But things are different, now that the hotel has asked for help in constructing avalanche defences on the south slopes of the Kreigerspitz. They want to erect the steel fences this summer, so that they can plant the woodland in the autumn.'

'The hotel's position looks a perfect site to me,' Dirk said.

'They'll erect the snow-bridges this summer – they are sparing no expense. The steel uprights will be concreted into the ground. Half-way through the project, the promoters will say they can't afford to finish the job – and the canton will insist on the village contributing towards the cost. Up will go the rates again.'

The bitterness in Rudi's voice brought silence to the room. The flames flickered; the logs hissed and spluttered.

'They have been too clever for us. They've even managed to per-suade the weather research people – that new station in Kretchma's farm which you passed on your way down – to certify that an avalanche risk could exist. A lot can be achieved through expense accounts, especially if you can offer free dinners to those you want to bribe.'

'Hush, Rudi . . .'

Frau Strauss had put her arm round her husband's shoulder, as she held the glass of water for him. 'Take your pill, dear.'

'They're all in it,' he spluttered. 'We'll have to help, just as I told the council . . .'

'Has Herr Trevallack ever seen round a *seilbahn*?' Anna interrupted.

'I'm sure papa would like to show him over it. . . .' The older man was jerked from his cantankerous mood. His blue eyes lit up. 'Any time you like. Glad to show you round, Herr Dirk . . . anything else I can do?'

Dirk relished the warmth in the compliment. Rudi must be at least twenty years older.

'Thanks, Herr Rudi. Could you lock up our money for us, if you have a safe? And I'd very much like to see your station but we've a lot on tomorrow. We're determined to try those pistes. We want to hire our skis tonight, so we don't waste time tomorrow. We've only got our *langlauf* skis and I'm itching to ski downhill again. D'you know the best shop, Herr Rudi?'

In the discussion that followed, Dirk watched husband and wife muttering together while their children discussed the merits of the hire shops. Rudi leaned across to Kim and smiled, the corners of his eyes wrinkling in kindness: 'Hans and Anna are leaving on Monday,' he explained. 'Their room will be vacant, if you would care to have it.'

Dirk glanced across at Kim. Her face was glowing with contentment and from the heat of the fire. Her eyes met his momentarily. Before he could reply, she had spoken for them.

'If you're sure that Hans and Anna don't mind . . .'

Dirk felt the leap in his heart. He glanced across at her, unable to absorb the promise behind her words. He rose to leave. 'Thank you' Herr Rudi. There is nowhere we would rather stay.' He held out his hand for Kim.

'We must hire those skis, before it's too late.'

They walked in silence to the ski-shop. Their gear would be ready for them in the morning.

'I've bought you a present,' she said. 'You can be tidy now.' She held up the yellow ski-bag for him to see. 'You can transfer your things tonight, ready for tomorrow.'

It was a sturdy, ample pouch, suitable for the emergency kit he always carried: screwdriver, leather laces, lip salve, polaroid glasses – there was even room for the length of rope and the karabiner shackles which that rascal Berlini had insisted they took for their frontier crossing – and they ought to have their passports franked tomorrow at the police station, after trying to get rid of the codes. He leaned down and kissed her on the cheek 'I'll even buy you a slivovitz, if you can manage one.'

The bar was warm and cheerful with its red-clothed table tops. She slipped her anorak from her shoulders, shook her flaming curls free. She nestled contentedly against his shoulder while they waited for the drinks. He had not been so happy since Judy, over four years ago . . .

'Dirk?'

'Uh?'

'I took a look round the weather station, while you were having your wound fixed up at the farm.'

'Strange place, wasn't it?' He slipped his arm around her waist.

'There was a large computer thing in the new building,' she said. 'The weather records are evaluated there, Rudi told me. He believes that the station receives reports from all the minor weather posts in this region of the Alps. Apparently, the staff are always out reading their local instruments, even in the worst of weathers. A computer takes a lot of power and that's why they have the big generators.'

'And there was an explosives store. I could just see the labelled boxes through the window.'

'Don't fret yourself, Kim,' he said. 'The rescue services often use them in the mountains.'

Her mood changed and she detached herself, adding irritably: 'Stop treating me as a child. I haven't finished yet. There was another window at the back, in the dark bit under the trees . . . '

The waitress was approaching with their drinks. Kim changed the conversation towards tomorrow's plans and to the days left ahead of them. First, contact the bank's representative at the Schreckhorn Hotel. Once they had unburdened themselves of the cash and the codes, the heavens could fall down on them, for all Dirk cared. Antony Rice, Henderson had said over the phone, was working on the bank's behalf. He was a communications expert and had been warned to expect their arrival.

'Can't wait for Monday,' Dirk said, downing his drink. He put his arm around her again.

She pressed the bundle about his waist. She glanced up at him, took his hand in hers. He paid the bill and they walked back to the *seilbahn*, their arms about each other. At the corner of the road leading down to the cable-car, he pulled her gently into the shadows. He put his arms about her and kissed her fully on the lips. She did not resist but tucked herself into the comfort of his body.

He knew now, after these difficult days, that he could not do without this girl. Their sudden awareness of each other had been no lightning flash; rather, a stealing into each other's hearts through the gradual appreciation of each other's qualities. As she responded to his kiss, a sense of protectiveness swept through him; he longed to cherish this woman, eradicate the heartache lurking behind those mysterious hazel eyes. He pressed her head into the warmth of his anorak.

'I've known it all along,' he said. 'I've been fighting the inevitability of it. I thought you meant to guard your independence. When you accepted the Strauss's suggestion, that changed everything.'

She reached up and pulled down his face to hers. 'I've given up struggling,' she whispered in the darkness. 'I love you. That's all I know.'

She was trembling when finally they stood apart to face each other.

'You're shivering,' he said. 'We'd better go in.'

'The Strausses have been so good. We mustn't keep them up. But, Dirk . . .'

'Yes?'

'I never finished telling you about the farm.' She laid her head on his shoulder and spoke quietly in the darkness.

'That window on the north side of the new building: it was set higher than the others – to catch the light better, I suppose, because it was under the trees. Curiosity drew me to it, so I dragged an empty wooden crate to the base of the wall. I was scared, in case your farmer friend caught me out. . . .' Dirk could feel her tenseness, as she hesitated, nervous perhaps of ridicule.

'Go on, Kim.'

'I stepped up on to the box. I cautiously raised my head above the sill. It was very dark inside. The reflections of the window panes made it difficult to see. Gradually, I took in the details, absorbing the proportions of the sombre room. Suddenly, a waxen woman's face was watching me, almost touching the window pane.'

Her arm tightened about him, as she forced herself to continue:

'Two sightless eyes were staring through me – like a corpse's. I tried to stifle my scream. I sprang down from the box and when I reached the gate to wait for you, I was shaking all over. It was horrible, Dirk.'

He held her close, trying to comfort her. Gently, he led her towards the door of the Strauss's house.

'So that was why you were so pale. Whoever it was, did she see you?'

'I don't know,' she whispered. 'I'll never forget those blind, glazed eyes. Her face was an old woman's, but her hair was blonde. She could not have been more than thirty.'

The lowering clouds had obliterated the stars and it was bitterly cold. She was shivering in the darkness as he rapped on the door.

Chapter 14

Sunday, 25 January, began dismally, a cold, grey day with thick cloud enveloping the lower slopes of Schreck. As Dirk and Kim left the village for the new road leading across the bridge to the Schreckhorn Hotel, they passed groups of disconsolate skiers trying to while away the morning, in the hope that conditions might improve for the afternoon. All the Zieger Joch and Krabach Kopf lifts and runs were closed. In the valley visibility was down to two hundred metres – it was nil on the slopes.

They had collected their skis and left them at the *seilbahn*, safe with the Strausses. They had donned their touring boots and were slithering up the road winding through the dark pinewoods which guarded the Schreckhorn valley. Passing a clearing where a forester was feeding a herd of deer, they rounded a hill, studded with rock and pines. The silence and the gloom of the wood pressed upon them, as their footsteps crackled upon the ice. They had spoken little and were glad to emerge into the light of the valley. They had spruced themselves up for this, the final lap of their adventure, but Kim felt dowdy in her skiing gear, if she had to face the critical scrutiny of a luxurious hotel. 'To hell with them,' Dirk had teased her when they met for their coffee and rolls. 'What's it matter, once we've delivered the goods?'

A man in dark green overalls stepped silently from behind a mound of snow-capped rocks. He wore an ear-muffed fur hat and his breath steamed as he halted them. The monogram, 'sh', was embroidered on the breast pocket of his uniform.

'This is a private road,' he announced in broken English. 'For hotel guests only.' The metal fillings in his teeth glinted as he smiled courteously. 'May I see, pliss, your passes?'

'Herr Rice,' Dirk said briskly. 'We have an appointment with him.'

'Your name, sir?'

'Trevallack.'

The guard extracted a walkie-talkie from his hip pocket. There was a short, guttural conversation and then they were being firmly escorted up the approach road. A horse-drawn sledge, its bells tinkling, swept past them, its runners screeching on the ice, as the driver, perched high on his seat, battened down the brake for the hill.

'We don't allow cars,' the guard muttered. 'We fetch our guests from the station.'

They rounded a bend and the hotel appeared, a four-storied, gargantuan chalet in split-levels. The walls were of stone; the low pitched roofs were mantled in snow; the pine-wood shutters were drawn back for the serried rows of dark windows to stare down secretively upon any approaching visitor. The guard handed over his charges to the fur-coated doorman who was stamping his feet at the top of the flag-stone steps. He saluted and held open one of the glass doors. They stamped the snow from their boots and went into the entrance hall.

Dirk crossed over to the receptionist who was watching them from behind her oak desk.

'*Guten Morgen,*' he began tentatively. 'Are you expecting any English soon?'

'No, sir.' Her eyes were hard above her brittle smile.

'No others?' He felt irritated. He turned his back, needing time to think. An attractive blonde, with hair curling about her shoulders, was watching them from the distant bar. Her superb legs were crossed seductively where she sat at the bar on the high stool, her solid-looking partner by her side. 'No, sir. No other English guests . . .' the receptionist repeated.

'When is Mr McHuish arriving?' he asked, turning round again. Kim was tweaking at his sleeve.

'I regret we are forbidden to disclose our guests' arrangements.'

'Thanks for your help.' He raised his voice and his anger showed.

'Can I help?' The warmth of a stolid, Yorkshire accent was hailing from behind him. 'Mr Trevallack, isn't it?'

A swarthy man of about thirty-five was striding across the hall. He was wrapping a red scarf about his neck and was zipping up his anorak, as he clumped in his ski boots across the hall.

'The forester told me you were on your way.' He smiled and held out his hand. 'All right, Ingrid,' he called to the girl behind the desk. 'I'll take care of them.'

He led them to an alcove and shook Kim by the hand. 'Tony Rice,' he said, lowering his voice. 'Mr Henderson has told me something about you.' He looked about him, glanced at a child's sledge from which sprouted an attractive arrangement of blood-red poppies and dried summer flowers. 'We can't talk here.' The flaxen-haired girl was setting down her Martini to stare at them.

'I'm snatching a couple of hours,' Rice said. 'The visibility is improving. I'm itching to try my new skis. Care to join me?' He seemed taut and ill at ease, but his bonhomie returned as soon as they climbed into the sledge waiting for them at the bottom of the steps.

He talked of nothing but Schreck and its ski runs for the duration of the trip down to the village. The cloud had lifted and streams of skiers were bustling towards the lifts. 'They'll just manage the Krabach red run before lunch,' Rice said. 'We ought to be back by one. We'll take the Krabach Kopf cable-car. You can pick up your skis while I get the tickets.'

They rejoined him in the *seilbahn* and, as the packed cabin slowly slid from the wooden platform, Dirk glimpsed Rudi Strauss behind the glass window of his control room. The Austrian's eyes were glued to his instrument panel. He was oblivious to the jostling skiers, laughing and shouting in the orange cabin which was now swinging from beneath the overhanging roof of his station.

'It's a thousand-metre lift to the restaurant at the summit,' Rice shouted. 'We're at 1420 metres here. They call the half-way pylon the Axe, because of the overhang. It's just over 1700 metres – nearly five and a half thousand feet, if you prefer British limits.' They joined him in the space he had saved for them at the rear window.

Dirk was unused to these Alpine cable-cars. The cabin bumped over the lower pylon, two hundred yards from the *seilbahn* and then it swung off into space. He tried to subdue this secret fear of his, but he detested the constriction in this aluminium box.

He looked down upon the ants crawling across the slopes beneath them. The car was travelling fast, swinging gently from side to side in the breeze that was slapping at the perspex windows. The bights of the driving wires, a quarter of the size of the suspension cable, were looping and swaying behind the orange cabin as it swished along the cable spanning the void between the Axe and the *seilbahn*.

A shadow flicked past, as No. 1 cabin flashed by, on its way down, barely five metres away. Then the whirr of the suspension wheels decreased as the rate of ascent slowed down.

'We're approaching the cliff of the Axe,' Rice said. 'It's almost a vertical lift here. This bit always worries me, when I look through the front.' His laugh was brittle. 'That's why I like the rear window.'

By standing on his toes, Dirk could see over his neighbour's shoulder. The rock face was charging towards them at an alarming rate.

'There's the Schreckhorn Hotel.' Kim was pointing down at the track leading between the hills and through the woods. 'What a fantastic site it has all on its own and tucked away at the foot of those slopes.'

Rice remained silent, peering through the side window. The last of the tree-line was sliding away beneath the cable-car; in a hollow below the snow-laden pines, nestled Walther Kretchma's farm.

'We called in there yesterday, on our way down,' Dirk said. 'That's the aerial of the weather station.' He had to peer past the nape of Rice's neck. The man was silent, intently watching the farm as it slipped behind the pines. He remained with his back to them as the car swooped up the last few metres of the cliff face. Dirk watched, his heart in his mouth, as the rocks rushed towards the leading edge of the cabin floor.

The cable-car swooped suddenly, the suspension wheels rattling overhead as the cabin traversed the pylon. The car rocked, then took up a slow, pendulum swing as it continued its headlong rush up the second half of its journey.

'No. I jumped off its wheels here last year,' Rice said. 'The wind got up.'

Dirk was overawed by the grandeur of the scenery, as the car swung across the upper snow valley. Far distant, the Axe was already a pygmy triangle of orange steelwork. Schreck village was out of sight, but the hotel was still visible on the far side of the valley. Above those southern slopes towered the Kreigerspitz; its twin sister, the Zeiger Joch, was only a few kilometres to the eastward. He could still see the ski-schools snaking into the woods and down the Zeiger runs.

The car was crawling the last few yards into the quay of the station at the summit of the Krabach Kopf. The cabin operator swung back the doors, and then the passengers clumped across the wooden floor to the reception hall. 'We'll put on our skis at the top,' Rice said. 'We have time for the red run, if you hurry.'

It was grey and cold when they put on their skis. Wisps of snow were swirling across the timber platform of the viewpoint facing the mountain range. The Schreckhorn, aloof in its solitude, looked down upon its neighbours. Its twin peaks, jagged and cruel, reared majestically, and were just visible through the lowering cloud.

'All set?'

Rice led off, slowly at first, not sure of his companions. At each crest, he waited for them and then, as they lost height, the sun broke through. As they skied down, he began talking about himself.

He had been appointed British Bank's communication and liaison officer since the conception, under the strictest secrecy, of the European Community's grandiose scheme to adopt a common monetary system. He had been at the Schreckhorn Hotel for over a year, ever since it had been selected as the venue for the assembly of the Community's top banking brains.

'You can see the hotel now,' he said, as he side-slipped to a stop in a shower of snow. 'Looks the perfect site, doesn't it, isolated and, when there's sun, a veritable Arcady?'

Dirk nodded, unsure of Rice who was taut and ill at ease.

'How did you get the job?' Dirk asked bluntly, ignoring the small talk. Rice had given no clue yet that he knew of the existence of the codes.

'My wife comes from the other side of those mountains,' Rice said. 'She's Austrian, a good secretary and we can both speak the language. Without her, we would never have been ready on time for the inaugural ceremony.'

'When's that?' Kim asked innocently. 'We've an appointment with Mr McHuish when he arrives.'

Dirk was watching Rice, but he gave no sign. He was prodding the ice with his stick and staring at the snow.

'The opening ceremony is on Wednesday. They're laying on a colossal lunch for the VIPs. For the lesser fry, there's the Farmers' Supper tomorrow night.' He turned to them, a sour smile twitching at the corners of his mouth. 'Henderson said you two are working for BB; that's good enough, if you'd care to come along too.'

'Thanks. Okay, Kim?'

'Good. Seven, tomorrow night, then. It's a high old jamboree, so come in anything you like. Meet you in the bar.'

He was leaning on his sticks, staring across at the isolated hotel, his forehead creased in concentration. 'I'll be glad when it's all over,' he burst out suddenly. 'You've no idea what it's been like, organizing this vast communication network. BB took on the responsibility for all the UK banking groups, but they've given me no extra help. I've had all that – and now. . . .' He turned to them, his brown eyes searching, restlessly inquisitive. 'I'm glad you've come. Things are moving too bloody fast. May I call you Kim and Dirk? I've got to talk to someone I can trust.'

'Go ahead,' Dirk said. 'We know what it's like, being on your own.'

A light flickered for several seconds across Dirk's vision, so bright that it dazzled him. Tony Rice went rigid, then spun around towards the hill to their right. He jabbed his sticks into the snow.

'Follow,' he yelled over his shoulder. 'Fast as you can. Stay close.'

He skied down at a furious pace and did not check until he had reached the head of the Edelweiss run, the hotel's private lift which ran down through the trees to the river. On the far side, a T-bar led up the nursery run to the foot of the hotel's southern entrance. Rice was breathing hard and his face was flushed. Though he was in a hurry, Dirk resented his brusqueness.

'Can't stop. I'm breaking off here. Follow the red run down and take your time back to Schreck. Watch out for the cliff by the gully. There's ice there, but it's the only bad bit.' He hesitated, embarrassed by his inexplicable behaviour.

'Okay,' Dirk said patiently. 'See you tomorrow, at the Farmers' Supper. You all right, Tony?'

The man had lost his colour and his eyes kept straying to the pine-topped hill behind them. He nodded, then attempted a smile. 'Can't talk now. If anyone stops you, you haven't seen me. Got it? *You haven't seen me.*' He skied off down the hill as if the devil was behind him.

Chapter 15

Rudi Strauss had been in charge of the Krabach Kopf *seilbahn* for over nine years, so there was little he could learn about the weather. Their alarm clock had shrilled half-an-hour earlier and when he had seen the depth of snow against their neighbour's doorway he stole back to the comfort of Marthe's arms for a few more minutes. But he must start the day now: though the Shreckhorn and Krabach Kopf runs would be closed, Wendelin would be rapping on the door in twenty minutes for the first lift of the day – the provision trip for the Krabach Kopf restaurant.

Rudi had known worse cabin operators than Wendelin Geiger. He was reasonably reliable and two years ago had begun full of promise. But like so many youngsters today, he lacked staying power. It must have been last October that he had grown into the sullen young man that he now was. Rudi would have to take up the matter with the office, for the job was a vital one. One moment of carelessness – and it would not be only Geiger who would be out of a job.

He wiped the lather from his chin, sluiced his face and put the coffee pan on the stove. Marthe would finish the breakfast preparation – she would have his coffee steaming hot and ready for him, the moment the first trip reached the top.

Life would not be so peaceful in six days' time, the worst Sunday of the year, Championship Sunday when the week-enders came up from Innsbruck and the Bavarians from across the border. He hunched his shoulders and stepped out into the cold as he heard Wendelin at the doorway.

It was the yellow scar running across the bridge of Geiger's nose and biting into his right cheek that made this twenty-three-year-old seem nearer thirty. In this intense cold, the scar was uglier than usual.

''Morning, Wendelin. No customers today.'

Wendelin did not look up from the churns he was manhandling through the doorway to the lift. Four of these would be ample for today: the restaurant had topped up yesterday. 'You'll wait for the manager and Klothilde?'

'I'll let you know when they're here,' Geiger growled.

Rudi turned his back and climbed slowly up the stairs for another day's stint in the control room. In the passage way, he met the Englishman, already dressed and shaved, coming down from the attic room.

'Morning, Herr Dirk. Sleep well?'

Trevallack was more at ease than he had been last night. He and his woman had returned early in the evening and had been much more reticent. On Saturday, their first night, they had come back late from their evening stroll and Marthe had made allowances for them. 'It's good to see two people in love like this,' she had said, taking Rudi's hand. 'Brings back memories. . . . But I'll say something to them dear, if they're too late again.'

'Slept like a log, Herr Rudi,' Trevallack said.

'You can move into our daughter's room, as soon as you like. They're leaving after breakfast, if the pass is cleared.'

'Thanks. There'll be no lifts open today?'

Rudi shook his head. 'It's snowed all night – over a metre. A blizzard has been blowing across the peaks. The wind's dropping but will soon get up again. I won't be able to use the *seilbahn*, so, if you wish to see my station, I could show you round.'

After breakfast, the anemometer was showing gusts of between forty-five and fifty-five kilometres an hour and Strauss shut the Krabach Kopf lift.

'Can't operate in this, Herr Dirk. I've been lucky to have got down the restaurant staff.'

Trevallack was fascinated by the mechanics of the station. The weather was so foul, that Rudi gave up the morning to a tour of inspection: he could carry out his lubrication routines at the same time.

'The woman will look after your things and change the rooms. We'll start down in the motor room and work our way up. It's always colder in the basement, where the main electric cables come in.'

They clambered down to the basement where Rudi began his tour: 'Two electric motors for driving the hoist wires – one motor can lift five persons. By coupling up the motors in parallel, I can lift the maximum car load of twenty-five people – including Wendelin.' Then he added apologetically: 'My *seilbahn* has been running for fifteen years, averaging sixty to seventy trips a day. At this pressure,

I have two operators working from nine in the morning to three in the afternoon; then from three to six. It's a long day, and a tired operator is a hazard we can't risk.' He moved to the doorway. 'We won't waste time in the switch-gear room, but go straight up to the second storey: that's the machinery room you can see through the glass window when you board the cabin – the room where the drive-wheels turn.' He ushered Dirk into the large space where his machines glistened, spotlessly clean as a result of the way he lovingly maintained them.

He could not conceal his pride as he explained the system: 'In two years' time, if Schreck continues to expand, they'll be investing in a new *seilbahn*. They'll have to rebuild our house, because the new cars will lift fifty persons a trip.'

'What's the weight of those enormous clumps of lead balancing the suspension cables?' the Englishman asked.

'140 tonnes on each. The cables are anchored at the summit and the stretch is taken up by these weights. The cables are inspected photographically every two years and are replaced if necessary. They have to be virtually unbreakable, because they take the entire weight of the system.'

'What about the drive-cables?'

'They're much smaller, because they need only haul a loaded car upwards along the suspension cables. The wires heave at speed round the big driving-wheels which are driven by those twin DC electric motors. But however hard we try, there'll always be accidents. Remember last year in France?'

'What happened?'

'The uphaul broke on No. 2 cabin. The electro-magnet automatic brakes failed to operate. The cabin slithered downwards over a thousand metres before crashing into the *seilbahn*.'

'Did they ever discover the cause?'

Rudi shook his head: 'It's difficult to know the physical effects on metal of the extreme cold of these winter nights. It's bad enough in the cabins: you'd be lucky to survive a night – imagine what the cold is like when there's a wind. . . . Here is our emergency brake.' He touched the relay which was automatically operated by the cut-outs in the control room.

'If we have an electrical power failure,' he went on, 'these are the emergency diesel generators. They give a rate of descent of only one metre per second; under normal conditions, the cabins travel at seven metres a second – and the two cabins do the trip in just under seven minutes.'

It was snowing hard when they reached the large window opening on to the cabin which was waiting in the station. The white flakes were whirling past, obliterating everything.

'It's a blizzard, all right – one of the worst we've had this winter. They've rung up from the weather station: over a metre of snow in twenty-four hours. Not good.' In his imagination, Rudi recalled the terrible memories of 1951. Those twisted, crushed bodies, the putrefying corpses when the snows melted in the spring.

'What's the danger?' Trevallack asked naïvely. 'Broken legs when the skiers leave the pistes?'

Rudi stared through the window. 'The snow's unstable,' he said. 'They'll close the runs.' He would not unsettle Trevallack. What could he know of the terror and of the irresistible destruction of the *lawine*?

'This is my control console,' he said briskly; 'this the foot-brake; this, my "dead-man's handle".' He pointed to the distance gauge on the right, which indicated on its scale the two positions of the cabins as they swung along the suspension cables – an indispensable aid when the mountain was blotted out by sudden snow storms.

'What about communications?' Trevallack asked. 'Can you talk to the cabin operator, as well as to the summit station?'

'There's a phone in the cabin, but this arrangement is no good: the static electricity caused by the wheels running on the main cables often blanks out conversation when I'm running at speed. The new cabins will have better communications.'

He glanced at his interrogator who was submerged in the technical details. He had no idea of the peril facing Schreck if this blizzard continued. The official warning had been promulgated: a state of general danger already existed.

There was always an 'if', she supposed. *If* only Dirk was not so concerned by the seed of suspicion that Rice had implanted this morning; *if* only she had not recognized those men waiting nonchalantly at the bottom of the run, when Dirk and she had reached the foot of the Krabach Kopf red run yesterday. There was that blonde they had seen in the Schreckhorn bar – and her big companion had been the ill-mannered brute who had kicked them out of the farm on Saturday. He was still wearing those dark glasses, and

99

he took little notice when Dirk and she had skied past them. And *if* their only contact with BB had been a more stable character – the continuing responsibility of the codes was getting Dirk down.

They had decided not to trust Rice with their secret. They would wait first to see what the Farmers' Supper might produce. Rice might even open up a bit. Whatever happened, tomorrow night McHuish was due . . . but tonight she was determined to forget the worries of this extraordinary day. She had enough time for a bath, before Dirk returned from his tour of the village – he had an obsession that their arrival had not gone unnoticed. She would try to make him forget his worries – but he was reticent about their new-found intimacy, now that they were expected to share this night together.

The Strausses had been fantastic with their hospitality – and she lay in contentment in the hot water, letting the tiredness flow from her limbs. Frau Marthe had treated them both as one of the family, considering them as married . . . and she, Kim, had no shame for this, their newly-discovered love. She longed for the coming night – and to hell with the sinister complications that were besetting them. She slipped out of the bath, glanced in the mirror, smiling to herself. She could still feel his hands upon her when, last evening, they had snatched an hour to themselves. He had whispered, then, of his love for her, of how he longed for tonight. They had waited so long for each other.

Chapter 16

Franz Freissiger stood in the centre of the entrance hall with Anastasia, his beloved companion and wife for seventeen years, and mother of his children, by his side. She was a picture in the lime-green velvet gown, her sallow, placid face illuminated by that disarming smile of hers as she greeted their 'guests', as they liked to be called.

Together they had started in the hotel business fifteen years ago, whilst she was still carrying little Bertha, their long-legged daughter now away at boarding school in Innsbruck. He had reason tonight to feel a smug satisfaction that the gamble of their lives had come off. He had borrowed more than he cared to remember to launch this Schreckhorn Hotel. His co-directors and the promoters had been hard taskmasters, but at last the enterprise was beginning to regain the capital invested.

'*Guten Abend* . . .' He smiled at the sea of faces filing past him on their way to the dining-room. The Farmers' Suppers had been a brilliant idea of Anastasia's: they were now part of the annual programme. The German customers revelled in the bucolic evenings: he even drove down himself to Brugfeld in his Volvo brake to bring back the best draught beer that the region could provide – worth doing, even though the pass could be closed at any moment in this terrible winter.

'One of our first guests,' Anastasia was murmuring. 'Tony, you'll be pleased to have some of your countrymen here this evening – and Mr McHuish will be here tomorrow.'

'It'll be pleasant, Frau Freissiger.' The Englishman smiled briefly. 'Time for a quickie before your speech?'

'*Ja, ja,*' and Franz nodded paternally. Herr Rice was a bag of nerves these days. On two occasions he had been drinking too much, but that was understandable: the fellow's work-load had been excessive to prepare for this most vital of conferences. The Minister for Tourism, with an unusual stroke of genius, had proposed that the conference should be held in Austria on neutral territory – the EEC had been bickering for months which country in the Common

Market should be the host; once the Austrian suggestion had been accepted, the Schreckhorn Hotel seemed a good choice. But the work had been hard and costly.

The Supper was fully booked: the tables had overflowed into the adjacent restaurant reserved for casual trade. Unfortunate, but there it was – Herr Rice had complained at being banished there, and Franz had spent too much time trying to juggle the places to fit him into the dining-room . . . and now the fellow had insisted on inviting two of his countrymen.

'I must go into the kitchen, *liebling*,' she whispered, touching his sleeve. 'I'm not happy about the boar's head. Wolfgang's in one of his moods.'

Being a top-class hotelier these days was not all bread and honey – and the brunt fell on Anastasia. It was she who provided the *cordon bleu* reputation and she who created the atmosphere of impeccable good taste throughout the hotel.

He nodded at Hermann, his unreliable but good-natured head waiter, who was approaching with the traditional hand-bell. The clanging momentarily broke the buzz at the bar. Those aloof scientists from the weather station were slipping from the high stools and gathering themselves together. He could not fathom that attractive blonde with the big Italian – or was he Sicilian? Whatever their function in Schreck, they had certainly brought their fair share of cash to the hotel, with their partiality for good living.

His eyes travelled around this room which Anastasia and he had so painstakingly created. 'One of the loveliest rooms in the hotel world', a top agency had described it – and he agreed with them.

He glanced at the fifteenth-century statuette his father had left him. The painted carving of St Hubertus stood in its niche in the central pillar. The saint carried an arquebus in one hand, while in the other he held high a golden cross – and each night Franz locked him away in the Schindler safe.

He strolled silently across the Persian carpets to make his presence felt in the bar and the far lounge. He bowed graciously to the smiling faces, to the well-to-do in their dinner suits; to those in the modern style of *après-ski* – and, when he could, he separated the latter in the adjoining restaurant for functions as important as these.

Sophie, his head barmaid who worked all hours for the pleasure of the job, was engaged as usual in hanging her delicious bosom over the crimson table cloths as she served the drinks. She smiled up at him, knowing her role perfectly as she discreetly urged the last-drinkers towards their food troughs. He was sure that she and her two helpers, all dressed alike in their bewitching *dirndls*, were part of the bar's soaring profits.

The room was emptying. The snug alcoves and their settles with the golden cushions which had cost over 100,000 schillings each, were vacant. Brunhilde, in her snow-white tunic, was locking up the door leading to the gymnasium and the sauna. She would open up the pool after the supper, in case there was a call for late-night roistering – a rare event in the Schreckhorn.

He turned and walked past the emptying bar. He felt for the draft notes in his pocket: he had practised his forthcoming speech in English – a courtesy that had gone down well with the Anglo-Saxons for the past three years. He touched a petal of one of the huge poinsettias in the copper tureens that had belonged to Anastasia's mother; he kicked at the undisciplined log which was smouldering on the edge of the flagged fireplace; he checked the lock of the precious seventeenth-century panelled cupboard, painted in Austro-Hungarian fashion in matt green, gold and red.

He strolled into the reception lounge again, where a young couple were hesitating in the porch, as they perused the restaurant menu. English by the look of them. He felt sorry for those people. It was obvious by the way they dressed that the disaster of the falling pound had killed that market. He always had been amused by the peculiarities of the race – but he found it difficult now to stomach the loud-mouthed Britons (and there were too many of them) who belly-ached of their country's misfortune and, at the same time, blamed all foreigners for its plight. Franz waited by the glass doors and smiled at the couple pushing their way through the doors. These would be Herr Rice's guests.

Though he was still burdened with the codes, Dirk Trevallack was enjoying himself for the first time in weeks. The gargantuan meal was over, he felt on top form from the slivovitz and draught beer – and Kim was by his side and nestling against him.

The evening had been a good one, in spite of Tony Rice's pugnacious attitude to all and sundry. He had drunk too much and was becoming a bore. From the very first, when Franz Freissiger had been forced to seat them in the restaurant, Tony had been impossible. His ego had been affronted and he vented his feelings on the fat American – and there were several here tonight, sloshing back the schnapps and walloping down the beer.

The band incident had set Rice going. The pleasant Austrian trio, accordion, drum and fiddle, had been pumping out the Viennese waltzes when a big American took over the accordion. A stein of beer quickly soothed the bemused instrumentalist who had been so roughly displaced.

The American set the pace, to the stamping of feet, the thumping of beer mugs and the singing of rollicking songs. And then the bandsman wanted to regain his place, to take up his accordion again.

At first, the joke was enjoyed by all, the big American getting all the laughs while the little bandsman tried feebly to wrest back his instrument. But when the Yank lunged out and sent the Austrian sprawling across the floor, the charade went sour. The accordionist picked himself up and stole out of the dining-room and into the restaurant. Forlorn and dejected, he sat down at the vacant table next to Kim.

Dirk tried to restrain Tony Rice who, now simmering with indignation, was climbing unsteadily to his feet. He side-stepped and ostentatiously bowed to the Austrian accordionist. Leading him by the arm, Rice threaded his way through the tables until he reached the band. Before the big Yank realized what was happening, the accordion had been restored to its rightful owner.

An embarrassed silence followed as Rice, swaying on his feet, rejoined Dirk and Kim. He was grinning with satisfaction as the musical trio stomped once more into Teutonic rhythm.

'I'm allergic to bullying,' he said, antagonistically returning the stares of the diners in the other room. 'Had too much of it recently.'

'You've done all right,' Dirk said. 'Most of the clientèle are on your side.' He was surprised at the hate which, like a mask, had clamped down upon Tony's face. His eyes smouldered as he swilled down his beer. He reclined against the red velvet back of the settee in the corner of the alcove, out of sight from the curious onlookers, as he spread wide his arms.

'I've got to talk to you, Dirk and Kim.' He was speaking urgently, but keeping his voice low. The narrow separating wall between the two rooms acted as a convenient screen. Dirk glanced across at Kim who had placed her hand on the tormented man's sleeve.

'You can trust us, Tony,' she said quietly. 'Go ahead. We'll help if we can.'

'You won't thank me for this. You're in the manure heap merely by being at my table, let alone talking with me.'

'Don't be bloody ridiculous. You've drunk too much.'

'That's right, but it clears my brain. Think better. . . . Take a look at that shower in there . . .'

'Which ones?'

Kim, without turning her head, was murmuring across the table: 'Who's that blonde, with her nasty-looking boy-friend? That's the brute who chucked us off the weather station. They keep on looking this way, staring at us.'

'They're watching us like hawks,' Dirk said. 'Pity you made such a spectacle of yourself, Tony . . . gives them a good excuse.'

'Keep on chatting together, you two,' Rice snapped. 'But listen to what I've got to say. It may be too late tomorrow. Things are moving too bloody fast.'

Dirk glanced at the excited Yorkshireman. He seemed pale but, apart from his flickering, frightened eyes, he was sane and sober enough. 'What things?' Dirk asked testily. 'And why "moving fast"? What's up?'

The whole scene was a weird dream. He and Kim carried on a desultory conversation, while they faced those uncouth bastards at their table in the nearby corner of the dining-room. He could not catch what the girl was saying, but there were spasmodic bursts of coarse laughter as the big, swarthy Sicilian held forth. He was still sporting his dark glasses, grotesque in this subdued lighting. A ruthless bastard, Dirk thought, but probably intelligent, with his domed cranium. His thick lips were continuously pursed and his teeth flashed when he smiled at the girl. And she, with her blonde hair curling into the hollow between her provocative breasts, had drunk her fair share, by the way she was pawing him.

There were two others at the table. The smaller, a thin man with an emaciated face, had been amongst the skiing party who had turned up at the weather station. The other, a thickset, large Arab in his thirties, Dirk had not seen before. Rice was talking briskly again from his corner: 'The big bastard is boss of that lot – Nereo Sciacca. He's a top Mafia boy, sent up here to do their dirty work. One of the nastiest rogues I've ever met. Ruthless and a killer. Erika, his blonde bitch, is little better – a sadist . . . and the thin chap's called Zydek, an Albanian and a paid assassin. The large Arab is an Iraqi and one of the top men in AGLA.'

'The Palestinian hi-jackers?' Dirk asked quietly. 'The gang that mowed down the school children at the airport?'

'Right. The Action Commando of the Liberation Army ... powerful, immensely resourceful, ruthless. Make a pretty partnership, don't they, ACLA and the Mafia? For once, their interests are common. The last thing they want is a strong European Community. That's why they're here.'

'Meaning?'

'A European currency, with a common monetary policy would destroy the money manipulators and speculators. The Mafia would lose billions, and, indirectly, so would ACLA who are supported by the Mafia. ACLA has another interest in destroying this effort to produce a common monetary policy. They need a weak, divided Europe. They can put the screws on us even tighter by squeezing the oil prices. The ACLA villian is called Khan. He has just arrived from over the border, like you did.'

'You sure of all this?' The party at the other table had demanded their bill. The girl was slinging her handbag across her shoulder. 'They're about to leave, Tony.'

'Sit tight. I'll do the talking, if they come over here.' He was sitting erect, tense, his fingers drumming on the table. 'Of course I'm certain. They've been watching the setting up of this conference for over a year, since not long after I was appointed. I'm almost certain what they're up to. That's why I'm telling you, in case anything happens to me.'

'They're coming over ...'

A muscle twitched in Rice's face. The group sauntered through the door of the dining-room. The girl, Erika, led the procession, with Sciacca close behind. The blonde had passed their table, when the Sicilian stopped. He looked down contemptuously at Rice, then deliberately undressed Kim with his insolent eyes.

'These your friends?' Sciacca snapped at Rice, his Italian accent breaking through his excellent English.

Rice nodded as he looked up, mesmerized by the man in the dark glasses. He was trembling and there was an abject appeal in his eyes. Dirk leaned across the edge of the table, feeling the bundle beneath his shirt. What the hell was this shower up to?

'Tell them not to believe all they hear in Schreck,' Sciacca commanded, still staring at Rice. He slipped a card, face down, on the table. He glanced at Dirk and Kim, then swept onwards with his retinue. In silence, Dirk watched them picking up their coats before making their exit through the glass doors. He felt the draught, saw the blizzard flailing across the dark rectangle.

Rice was grey with tension. He clutched the card in his hand, crumpling it savagely.

'What the hell's going on, Tony?' Dirk asked angrily.

'Shut up, for God's sake, Trevallack. Your life's in danger and so is your girl's. I'm certain I've bowled out their intentions – terrible, terrible, for all of us,' and suddenly he clasped his head in his hands.

'I can't explain here. I've got to show you something, before you'll believe me. Meet me at the top of the Edelweiss lift tomorrow – I can explain plainly enough then.' He was losing control and beginning to weep.

'Why don't you go to the police?'

Rice smoothed out the crumpled card. 'Read that,' he whispered. 'They've got my wife at the weather station – they've been holding her hostage for months. I know too much.'

Chapter 17

She became gradually aware of the dawn stealing through the opened shutters. He had opened the window, in spite of the intense cold, before finally they had fallen asleep in each other's arms. From the first moment, when she had stood naked before him, their love for each other had swept away the relative trivialities of the world – and of the Farmers' Supper. She was aware of him now, stirring against her as he awoke drowsily at her side. She turned to him and cradled his head between her breasts.

In this first glimpse of dawn, Tuesday, 27 January, a new life was beginning for them, an existence totally shared. She loved him, God, how she loved him – never again would she be so alone, as she had been during these last miserable years. She sighed with pleasure as she felt him searching for her with his first awakening.

They slept afterwards, drowsily awaiting the clatter of the household to rouse them from the comfort of their duvet. They enjoyed the breakfast with the Strausses, Dirk being relaxed for the first time in weeks, it seemed to her. It had snowed again during the night, a blizzard that had again obliterated all traces of the previous day. As they walked out into the cold of the morning, the sun broke through. The sky was blue, the cirrus high in the stratosphere – she took his arm and pressed his hand with sheer delight of living.

'Come on,' he said. 'We'll just make Tony's rendezvous in time.'

He carried her skis and clambered up the steps to Rudi Strauss's cable-car. Wendelin Geiger was not here this morning. A cabin operator she had not seen before slammed the aluminium doors behind them. The cabin heaved and they were sweeping upwards, away from the village which, so suddenly, was teeming with skiers forging their way to the lifts. At last, for so many frustrated holidaymakers, a sunny morning on the slopes was guaranteed.

At the Krabach Kopf summit, the ski-schools had already departed, the advanced classes to the black run of the Schreckhorn, the majority to the blue run which joined the Edelweiss chair-lift lower down.

'You lead, Kim. I enjoy watching you.' He followed her down

relishing the beauty of the woman who, so short a time ago, had given herself totally to him. In her slacks and red anorak, her hair flowing free in the warmth of this beautiful morning, she was a picture of grace as she swung into the turns, a flurry of snow at her skis. He had his work cut out to keep up with her.

Rice was waiting for them when they reached the head of the Edelweiss lift. It was 11.05, and he was glancing at his watch, impatient to be off.

'Thought you weren't coming,' he said. 'We've precious little time.' He moved over to the clump of pine trees standing below the shoulder of the hill which concealed Walther Kretchma's farm on the other side.

'We're safe here. Thank God we can talk.'

'Well, Tony, what's it all about?' Dirk asked, determined to fathom Rice's anxiety. 'You owe us an explanation.'

The communications official had taken off his black gloves and was pointing with his stick to the opposite side of the valley.

'See them all, the happy skiers, cluttering the pistes below the Zeiger Joch? They're out in their hundreds . . . See them there, below the snow-tractors clearing the runs?'

Dirk watched the orange machines, midget toys crawling across the pistes below the mountains. The chair-lifts to the summit were full to capacity as they carried their loads above the pine woods separating the Zeiger Joch from the Kreigerspitz.

'They'll be revelling in this,' Dirk said, 'after the frustrations of the last two days.'

'As long as the Zeiger runs aren't closed. It's safe enough there, but, with this snow and sudden warmth, the Schreckhorn black run may have to be shut.'

'Why?'

'Avalanche danger.'

Dirk glanced across the valley, where the sun was streaming upon the Schreckhorn snowfields and the southern flanks of the Kreigerspitz. On either side of the gully above the hotel, ant-like figures were working at the top of each snowfield, close below the Kreigerspitz summit.

'You've seen 'em?' Rice said. 'The weather men, crawling all over the mountains?'

'What are they up to?'

'Taking their readings to feed into their computer.' He added bitterly: 'Too bloody simple, isn't it? Sciacca and his gang have fooled the lot of us. I am *sure*, absolutely *certain* now, that I've got it right. You know, don't you, that in 1564, according to the records, the Kreigerspitz avalanched and destroyed the whole of the Schreckhorn valley, where the original village used to be?'

'Someone told me earlier. So long ago, that no one bothers . . .'

'Right. But supposing those conditions again existed, or almost existed, the hotel and *everyone in it* would be overwhelmed if an avalanche was sprung.' He was talking rapidly, his black gloves gesticulating excitedly. 'Ever since they came here, Nereo Sciacca and his boys have been working on it. Their ACLA computers confirmed the forecast that this could be a similar year to 1564, once the bad weather set in during November and December. And even if conditions did not exactly match up, it's easy enough these days to release an avalanche, once conditions are ripe.'

'D'you mean that Sciacca would spring that lot, those two huge snowfields above the hotel? Don't be absurd.'

'Not only *could*, but he *will* do so, as soon as the hotel is bursting with the Community's VIPs. He'll spring those two fields and the lot will hurtle down that central gully.'

'That's mass murder,' Dirk said. 'A bloody massacre.'

Dirk was too stunned for words. The hotel lay peacefully in the sun. It was hot and the guests, pygmies from here, were lolling in their *chaise longues* on the terrace, while swimmers splashed in the aquamarine-blue of the underground swimming-pool.

'Tomorrow there's the opening ceremony,' Dirk said. 'Anybody who's anybody will be there.'

'My God, Trevallack, you're swift off the mark.' Rice snapped. The appalling truth had numbed Dirk's thinking, but Rice was talking fast, his voice rising in desperation. 'What the hell can we do to stop it?'

'Go to the police; see the authorities.'

'They'll kill Greta. They'll murder her in cold blood.' His voice had sunk to a whisper. 'And if we go to the authorities, d'you expect they'll believe us? What proof have we?'

'They could raid the weather station; rescue your wife.' He knew his words were feeble, ridiculous. Greta Rice's life would be the price. 'We've *got* to go to the authorities,' Dirk said. 'We'll have done all we can.'

Rice laughed bitterly. 'D'you think they'd upset the village at this moment? They've spent thousands on advertising for the slalom championships.'

'When?'

'This week-end, thirty-first and first. The mayor would never over-rule the championship committee. An order to evacuate the hotel would cause panic in the village. Championship week-end – *kaput*.' He drew his fore-finger across his throat.

'We can't sit here waiting for Sciacca. I'll go to McHuish tonight, the moment he arrives.'

Rice turned, his eyes wild.

'I'll kill you first.'

He had slipped his hand into the pocket of his anorak. A pistol barrel glistened in the sunlight, its snout pointing at Dirk's chest.

'Put it away,' Dirk said. 'You're ill, man.'

Kim had slipped gently beside the demented man. She laid her hand on his shoulder. 'Tony,' she said calmly, 'we'll see this through together. We promise we won't risk Greta's life.'

Rice broke into uncontrolled weeping. He snicked on the safety-catch and slipped the gun back into his pocket.

'Come on, Tony. Take a hold on yourself.'

Dirk was watching the helio flickering across the valley from the working parties moving about below the summit of the Kreigerspitz. They were operating in two groups, each at the head of the two snowfields. Hidden here beneath the trees, Rice, Dirk and Kim were in a direct line with the flashing mirrors.

'There's only one solution,' Dirk snapped. 'We've got to rescue your wife. We have only today, if your assumptions are right.'

'How can you save her, you bloody fool?' Rice shouted, insane with worry. 'I've been trying to think of something for months.'

'I'm trained in this sort of thing, Tony,' Dirk said quietly. 'I was in the Royal Marine commandos.'

A momentary gleam flickered in Rice's eyes.

'You could rescue her – alive?'

'We can have a bloody good try. Better than doing nothing. But we've got to move fast. We need a telephone and we'll have to go to the authorities. We must get down to serious planning.' An idea was already gestating in his mind. 'Have you done anything yourself yet?'

'I've monitored their frequencies. If they mean to release the avalanche by explosion, they'll be using a short-wave transmitter to trigger the detonators.' His glance flickered back to those ant-like figures working below the Kreigerspitz. 'I can jam their transmissions – but that's all.'

'Okay. You press on, Tony, back to your office. It's time we took the initiative.' He shook Rice's shoulder. 'Come on, man. We'll bloody well stop Sciacca's game – but we'll rescue Greta first. We must not be seen together so get back to your office and wait for us. We'll arrive during the lunch-hour. We'll do a few runs on the Edelweiss before following you down.'

Rice was slipping his hands back into his gloves. Suddenly he was a man again.

'Half-past one at the hotel,' he said. 'Sciacca and Erika always lunch there, to collect information and to keep up with developments. They're *bound* to be there today. Be careful of the cliff . . .'

They watched him twisting and turning down the track leading through the darkness of the wood. He disappeared and Kirk felt Kim's hand on his sleeve.

'I'm scared,' she whispered. 'Something terrible's about to happen.'

Chapter 18

The security guard at Walther Kretchma's farm was something new. The officious Austrian, Geiger realized as he showed his pass, was certainly not from this area.

Wendelin was surprised by the intense activity in the farm – things must be moving to their climax. His summons to attend the emergency meeting had arrived less than an hour ago: it was fortunate, that Tuesday was his day-off since Strauss was becoming impossible these days . . .

He walked briskly through the farmyard, past the wireless mast, to the assembly room on the ground floor. Joe, the engineer, was working on the emergency generators.

'Great to see you, Wendelin. It's not often that the whole team's here.'

'Everyone?'

Joe nodded. 'The Boss – and Khan.'

'I'd heard he'd arrived.'

'Two days ago: from across the border. Berlini brought him.'

'It's the real thing, then?'

'Your guess is as good as mine. We've been working long enough for it.'

Wendelin Geiger suppressed the pang of remorse, but his conscience had had little difficulty in tolerating the enormous cash benefit with which he had been bribed for his services to Sciacca and his organization. With the money, Klara and he would be able to buy that ski-shop with the flat above it. Mercifully, she was away with her parents at the moment and he was a foreigner from the other side of the mountains.

He passed the communications room, saw the high-power transmitter which wireless the radio engineer was checking. Wendelin waved to Manfried, the cheerful helio expert, who was passing the time of day with the radio watchkeeper. Manfried glanced at his watch and the two men moved to the doorway. Geiger waited for them and together they strode down to the conference room at the end of the building. The restricted area at the back of the house was under guard now (another security man whom Wendelin did not recognize), so the three men had to pass by the long windows of the computer rooms. The white-overalled operator was sauntering round the room, hands in pockets and smiling at those who were gathering for the morning's assembly. The computer operator was the only individual excused from the meeting, by the look of things.

Geiger felt insignificant amongst these high-powered individuals. He slipped away from his companions and slid into a chair at the back of the room. The clock on the wall showed 10.57.

At 11.00 precisely, he felt the cold draught at the back of the room. He rose with the others to his feet, as the Boss entered through the far door. A dark man, an Arab by the look of him, was following closely behind Sciacca. The two men took their places at the raised table which stood below the wall map of the Schreckhorn range.

'Sit down, gentlemen.' Nereo Sciacca spoke in excellent English, the common language by which the cosmopolitan team communicated. He indicated to his companion the vacant chair on the right. As the Boss began his briefing, Wendelin studied the two men with whom he was now criminally linked.

Both of them had that indefinable quality of leadership. In other men, this mysterious magnetism would have been easier to recognize; but, with the common purpose of them all – an objective never precisely defined – the leadership which Sciacca had imposed was one of fear. The whole thing reeked of evil and there were moments when Wendelin longed to quit. But he was too deeply involved – any defection by any of the staff would exact instant reprisal; the operation was so monstrous that a callous killing to safeguard its security would be as nothing in the overall planning. Gustav, one of the original programmers, had lost his nerve last August. He had taken the black run of the Schreckhorn one afternoon. He had never again been seen. The crevasses on the glacier must have claimed him, it was said in the village. There had been no trace, not even of his skis.

'Mr Khan is a newcomer to most of you,' Nereo was explaining. 'He is my second-in-command and a specialist in escape techniques after our mission. He is a member of the ACLA staff and has planned several successful operations. He will inform you of your escape routes, once I have finished with tomorrow's final details.'

Wendelin heard the sign of relief whispering through the audience. It was to be tomorrow, then, all things being equal – after so many months of secrecy, tension, and careful planning.

'You'll draw your arms from the armoury this afternoon,' Sciacca continued in his silken voice, the tone of his speech, flat, unemotional, bored with the business. There had to be a thread of callousness running through the whole audience, but it was Nereo Sciacca who was the architect of this horrific crime.

'Mr Khan will route all of you, by different channels, to our Middle East HQ. There you will draw your balance of danger money . . .' Sciacca laughed shortly, 'once the operation is successfully completed.'

For a brief instant the mask of respectability slipped from the Sicilian's face. The cruel mouth, the ruthlessness, the callousness flickered in those dark eyes. He was searching his audience for the slightest hint of betrayal, irresolution. In comparison, Khan, sitting imperturbably by Sciacca's side, was meekness itself. There was something hideous about Sciacca – and Wendelin Geiger felt the tingling at the back of his neck which this monster always induced in him.

'Our computer confirms that conditions today are suitable for our purpose. It also forecasts with ninety-six per cent probability, that tomorrow will provide even better conditions.' The harsh laugh jarred again: 'And tomorrow should give us an even better chance of total success, gentlemen. The inaugural ceremony is due at midday. If there's another blizzard tonight, the probability becomes a certainty. If it's sunny and warm tomorrow morning, as it was today, I can promise you all an early and prosperous retirement until the end of your days.'

A snigger shivered like a breeze through the room. At that moment, the door opened and Zydek, the lean-faced strong-arm man who always accompanied the Boss, entered quietly. The uniformed security man who was following at his heels, removed his cap. Nereo nodded briskly at them both, then continued his briefing.

'And now gentlemen, I must be sure you all know your duties. Timing is vital. Each of you will stand up, as I call out your names, and tell me exactly what is required of you. I'll begin with my "Attack Party", those who have been selected to accompany me: Mr Khan, Miss Erika, Mr Zydek – and Mr Geiger. . . . On your feet, please, Mr Geiger. Tell us in detail what you have to do.'

Wendelin stood up, felt all eyes upon him. The adrenalin was pumping hard, as he opened his mouth to speak.

Chapter 19

'It's a quarter past twelve,' Kim said as she halted in a flurry of snow at the bottom of the T-bar at the top of the Edelweiss. 'Time for another run?'

He glanced at her, his woman, who was smiling with happiness, her cheeks glowing from the exertion of the fast run down from the top. It was good to have a few moments together before they grappled with the unpleasantness that lay ahead.

'Better get going,' he said. 'If we start now, we'll only just be in time at the hotel. We've got to go the long way round, remember?'

She turned to him. Her lips were cold in the wind that was rising with the cloud sweeping in from the westward. The sun had glimmered its last pale rays and the first flakes were falling.

'Keep up if you can,' he yelled over his shoulder.

He heard her laughter as he thrashed off downhill. His parallels were improving, probably with the sheer joy and relaxation of being alone with her. God, it was marvellous to love her so. The real thing, this time – and tonight she would be in his arms again. The trees were flashing past him and he side-slipped to check his pace before streaking on to the ice. where the piste narrowed to the pathway.

'Careful here,' he yelled over his shoulder. 'Coming to the cliff.'

Rice's tracks were still visible, two parallel lines fast disappearing beneath the coverlet of snow that was falling. Dirk pulled down his goggles – he could see the bumps now. He slowed down as the sharp curve of the cliff came into sight. Cautiously he side-slipped to the edge of the precipice: the track was barely two metres wide, and the bank to his right sloped up sharply, preventing further turns. Suddenly, Rice's tracks ran out. He halted, waited for Kim.

'Where do we go from here?' The path diverged on the far side of the bend, each route showing a red and black marking.

'Take Tony's tracks,' she said as she slithered beside him. 'We can't go wrong if we follow him.'

'Can you see them? Blowed if I can . . .'

Then they spotted the ruffled snow a few metres further on.

Several tracks originated from behind the cut-away of the bank above them. A patch by the cliff-edge was humped and disturbed, with jagged heel-marks poking through the fresh covering. Dirk cautiously approached the lip of the precipice which fell sheer to the rocks and the trees thirty-five metres below.

'Kim . . .'

'Yes?'

'Come here.'

She slid to his side. He pointed his stick. 'There . . . to the right.'

In silence, they skied on down, negotiating the treacherous path as best they could. The right-hand fork was arrowed to Schreck; the left-hand, a black run now, led also to the village.

'Stop here, Kim. We can climb back again, if we have to.' He descended alone, down the left-hand route, towards the dark hump sprawling in a deep drift. The body was almost invisible, its grotesque outline already covered by a film of snow.

He brushed away the covering. Tony Rice lay there, ashen grey with death, his limbs twisted savagely by his fall down the rocky precipice. The injuries were terrible, his face beyond recognition – but the side of his head was ripped open where it lay in the stained and bloody snow. Gently, Dirk tried to untangle the sticks and the broken skis from the stiffened corpse. Rice's right hand was rigid in the pocket of his anorak. Dirk felt inside, touched the cold steel. He forced apart the fingers and extracted the small automatic. He slipped it into his own pocket, then grappled again with the corpse. The face flopped across to the other side.

'God . . .' Dirk whispered.

A neat hole, the size of an Austrian schilling, the flesh charred at the edges, oozed in the skull above the ear. He allowed the body to tumble back into the drift. He kicked back the snow.

'Don't move, Kim.'

A wave of nausea swept over him. He reeled for a moment, dizzy from the shock. He groped his way back to her, where she waited, white with apprehension. He took her in his arms and pressed her head into his shoulder. He forced her round, away from the horror at the foot of the precipice.

They reached the junction of the red run. Only the hiss of falling snow-flakes disturbed the silence as they stood there, unable to speak. He took her by the sleeve and led her down the track, below the hill which concealed the weather station above them. They reached the edge of the wood and stood looking down at the village, grey and lifeless at this hour, the slopes deserted.

'He was shot at close range.'

She gave a little cry, choking back the sobs as she clung to him. 'I'd felt all along that something terrible was happening,' she whispered. 'What are we going to do? We're the only ones who know.'

He showed her the gun. The magazine was full, the safety-catch untouched.

'What are we going to do, Dirk?' she repeated, and he caught the hysteria in her voice.

He felt the shivering of her body, heard the chattering of her teeth. He glanced upwards through the trees: the farm was invisible in the greyness of the snowfall which was now obliterating their surroundings.

'Let's get on down.'

He forced her to lead, felt the cold prick of fear at the terror lurking behind him. Then they were clear of the wood, out on the open slopes, the familiar clanking of the lifts' music in their ears. In the distance, they heard the laughter of children.

They skied as fast as they dared and reached the village street. The sudden warmth and noise of the Zeiger café brought them back to the world.

'Two schnapps and two bowls of soup, *bitte* . . .'

He refused to talk until the slivovitz had begun to do its work. She leaned against him until the trembling slowly ceased. It was past three o'clock before they had reached a decision.

Rice was dead. They would have to risk Greta's life. They would go to the authorities after handing over the codes to McHuish who was arriving shortly. With his authority, the police would be forced to take notice. Even in this blizzard, they would have to search for Rice's body. When they found it, they would realize the terrible fate awaiting them all, unless they acted with vigour and urgency.

McHuish held the key. There was nothing they could do but to return to the Strausses and wait.

Rosalind Emma Dermott was feeling her years. The plane had landed at Innsbruck in a blizzard. Her lord and master, whom she had served for so long as personal secretary and aide, had insisted on booking the last flight out. The journey to Schreck had been a trying one, the Mercedes taxi only just succeeding in fighting its way through the pass before it was closed. They were here, safely, in this superb hotel, but she would prefer not to live again through those last few hours.

Mr McHuish had retired with one of his rare migraines. He would not be down for supper and no one was to disturb him. He needed strength for tomorrow – and at sixty-one he had to conserve his strength if he was to compete with these younger men overtaking him from behind. A hot bath would relax her and then she could dine serenely, glad to be alone.

She was unzipping her practical travelling clothes, when the telephone buzzed by the side of the bed.

'Mr Trevallack and a lady?' She tried to conceal the irritation in her voice. 'No, Mr McHuish is indisposed.' She hesitated: this must be the agent about whom McHuish had been so mysterious. 'After dinner? All right, I'm coming down.'

The face staring back at her from the mirror as she dabbed on the powder was lined and grey with fatigue. She would be thankful when the boss retired from the bank: she would go too, with honours and a generous hand-shake. Reluctantly, she pulled herself together, then took the lift down to the entrance hall where the guests were assembling for dinner.

'Mr Trevallack?'

The young couple were waiting for her on the settee. She introduced herself and the young man stood up, a travelling grip in his hand. She noted the disappointment on his face. Obstinate as a mule, one of those who could never accept 'no' for an answer – Mr Trevallack was colouring with anger.

'We've travelled across Europe, Miss Dermott, to hand our packages over to Mr McHuish. I am not leaving until I do so.'

'Come with me, please.'

She wanted no scenes here. Hurriedly she led the way back to the lift. Inside her room, she faced them, angry at the man's insistence.

'The President has a migraine. He does not wish to be disturbed. His priority is for tomorrow's ceremony.'

'Tell him I have the codes, Miss Dermott. If he won't see me, the responsibility is no longer mine. I shall hand them over to you. All I need is a receipt.' He was clutching at the last strands of his self-control.

'Wait here, please. I'll ask Mr McHuish if I can accept them.'

The President was dozing in his darkened room. She stood by his bed, expecting the customary short rebuke.

'Take the packages, Rosalind. Check them against that list in my brief case. Then bring the codes to me and lock them in the safe.'

'Thank you, Mr McHuish.' She had collected the check list and reached the door when the tired voice spoke again from the darkness.

'Rosalind, I'll see them in the morning, if they insist. Ten o'clock.'

She was smiling to herself as she returned to her room along the green-carpeted corridor. The chief had only reached his exalted position because of his firmness of purpose.

Trevallack and Mrs Quintan silently handed over the codes as she checked them against the list. They were all there – and the cash, bonds and certificates. She tapped out a receipt on her portable. She smiled at them, relieved there had been no further unpleasantness.

And then she listened to their incredible tale. She would miss her dinner, unless she could get rid of them.

'You're overwrought, Mr Trevallack. Worn out, exhausted. If all this is true, why don't you go to the police?'

'How can I?' the man shouted. 'I have no authority – nothing to show. They'd lock me up as insane.'

He stood up suddenly, grabbed her by the shoulders, shaking her roughly, until the girl forced them apart.

He slumped suddenly in despair on to the bed, his head clasped between his hands. The girl stood over him, tenderly trying to calm the hysteria.

Miss Dermott moved slowly to the door. She despised histrionics and instability in a man. She could do nothing about this suspected murder.

'Ten o'clock tomorrow,' she said. 'He'll see you then, I'm sure.' She smiled bleakly.

She accompanied them down to the entrance hall and watched them departing through the porch. Outside it was snowing, the flakes flailing horizontally across the entrance. She could hear the howl of the wind, feel the bitter cold of the blizzard when the glass doors opened and shut.

Chapter 20

'*Guten Morgen*, Herr McHuish.'

The President of British Bank summoned a smile for the head waiter who was closing the slats of the blinds on the windows. Though it was only 9.15, the sun had climbed up from behind the Schreckhorn mountain and the heat through the picture window was becoming overpowering. The glare hurt his eyes this morning, and so Rosalind's suggestion to lower the blinds had been most welcome. The dull headache that lingered after his migraine was almost gone: but his stomach was, as always, deranged. The second cup of black coffee had set him up, but he could not eat. He smiled across at his secretary where she waited at her breakfast table in the restaurant annexe. There was more protocol in Europe than ever there was in liberal Britain.

The ski-school was already massing outside, and he, too, had better start his day. . . . 9.20, Wednesday, 28 January, inaugural day. He felt a twinge of dissatisfaction because he had expected to meet their communications man, the bank's only contact here. Antony Rice had been a costly but necessary expense. He might have had the manners to welcome his employer, after so long a time lapse . . .

I'm getting old and cantankerous, he thought, as he rose from his table. He caught a reflection of himself in the window – a well-groomed, silver-haired senior executive who could only be a Scot. Modestly self-confident, he knew that he had achieved his ambition – and not many men of his generation could claim that distinction these days.

'You haven't forgotten your meeting with that couple, have you, Mr McHuish?'

Rosalind, efficient and neat as ever, was waiting to meet him. He put a paternal arm about her shoulder. 'I'll be down in a minute. Any sign of Mr Rice?'

She shook her head. 'The management can't understand it, sir. He never returned to the hotel last night.'

*   *   *

They had longed for this, their second night together. But the developments of the day and the anxieties of the morrow had come between them, as they feverishly gave themselves to each other.

They collapsed in sleep, lost in each other's arms. Then the dawn came and, with it, the passion that had eluded them earlier. Frantically they made love, snatching at the minutes slipping away from them. Then it was dawn and the day lay before them, challenging and terrible. They must go to the police and then up to the hotel to see McHuish.

As they stepped out into the cold, the first skiers were gathering outside the *seilbahn*.

The President of British Bank was a good listener, Kim was forced to admit. His silvery head, sun-tanned face and Savile Row suit seemed out of place up here in the mountains.

Dirk and she had been invited up to the President's suite. Dirk had insisted that they must speak in private without the assistance of Miss Dermott – and breathlessly, he had finished making his report. What effect, Kim wondered, had his impassioned plea had on the suave, imperturbable Scot sitting in the armchair before them? Mr McHuish was glancing at his watch.

'You talk of Mr Rice's murder, Mr Trevallack, but what proof have you or Mrs Quintan to show me? You ask me to act on this incredible theory of yours. I arrive out here and, within hours, you ask me to stake my reputation on cancelling this important ceremony which is due to take place in less than three hours time. Come, come, Trevallack, your story is not credible.'

Kim watched the distinguished figure rising from his seat. He turned his back and stared through the windows towards the slopes below the Kreigerspitz. His hands were thrust deep into the pockets of his dark pin-stripe suit, but Kim sensed that his intelligent brain had not entirely rejected Dirk's warning.

'True, Trevallack, you and Mrs Quintan have safely delivered the codes and the bonds. For this the Bank will show its appreciation. But this fantastic story of yours, this . . . this demand that I must force the management to evacuate the hotel – have you dreamed it up – are you out of your mind?' McHuish slapped the table in annoyance. 'Rice's disappearance – you are asking me to take this seriously. Where is the body?' He turned round impatiently. 'Really, Mr Trevallack . . .'

Kim saw the anger flushing Dirk's face. With a quick movement, he jerked the pistol from his pocket and slammed it on the table in front of McHuish.

'This was in Rice's pocket. D'your communications people usually carry guns?'

McHuish stared at the metallic-blue steel of the weapon. Dirk continued angrily: 'I went to the police on my way here, because you would not see me, sir. They've been out searching for Rice's body, while the weather remains fine.' He laughed bitterly, as the phone purred by McHuish's side. 'And you ask for proof.' Kim pulled at Dirk's sleeve as he jumped up to go.

'Hang on, Trevallack; the police are downstairs.' He spoke quietly into the instrument. 'Yes, please, ask him to come up.'

The grey uniform, the peaked cap and the jackboots always seemed sinister, Kim thought. The *polizei* sergeant, a parcel tucked beneath his arms, had removed his cap. The hotel proprietor, Franz Freissiger, who was hovering in the background, acted as interpreter.

'The police sergeant is seeking your help, Herr McHuish, as you are the most important Englishman here. . . .' Kim watched the Scot wincing with annoyance. 'They have found the body of Herr Rice at the bottom of a precipice. The *polizei* are convinced he was murdered.'

McHuish nodded. 'You have proof?'

'The sergeant needs to establish identification.' Freissiger turned to the policeman. 'They found a clue on a ledge not far away from the corpse. Rice had been shot at close range through the head.'

The sergeant unwrapped the paper parcel. On the table, its fingers still curled and stained by melted snow, lay a black right-handed ski-glove. The insignia 'ws' was stamped in white upon the back of the leather. Below this motif of the weather station, three black letters had been added: 'ZDK'.

Chapter 21

For the first time in days, Dirk felt a tinge of hope. The identification of the ski-glove had a miraculous effect upon the select gathering in the President's suite.

McHuish took charge. Adding his authority to Dirk's rapid re-telling of the drama, he stirred even the sergeant into action.

'I am prepared to accept Mr Trevallack's improbable warning,' McHuish said. 'If you don't evacuate the hotel, Herr Freissiger, I shall take the matter into my own hands. A day's postponement of the ceremony is not the end of the world.'

Dirk felt sorry for the distraught hotel proprietor. Freissiger showed his dignity as he glanced about him; then he shook McHuish by the hand.

'*Ja*, I understand,' he growled. 'First, I will see my wife. We must have no panic, *nein*? She will see to the staff. I will stand by to clear the hotel of the guests.'

Dirk glanced at his watch: a quarter to twelve.

'What about rounding up the criminals?' he asked. 'Can the police act at once, even on this flimsy evidence?'

Freissiger did his best to shake the sergeant as the minutes ticked by, but the *polizei* representative stolidly shook his head. 'He'll have to obtain approval from headquarters,' the hotel proprietor explained.

'That's up to them,' McHuish snapped. 'Our responsibility is to the conference and to the hotel. Let's start in the bar. You'll help, Trevallack?'

'Of course.' Dirk glanced at Kim who was gripping his hand. 'But it's Sciacca I want; him and all his gang.'

They left Franz Freissiger and the policeman in the hall.

'I must socialize before the ceremony,' McHuish said. 'I'll spread the word quietly at the bar. Join me for a drink?'

Dirk felt desperate. The police had promised they would call him for the attack on the weather station – but how long would that be? Greta Rice's life was hanging in the balance. If they could not rustle up an armed force and a helicopter in time. . . . He took Kim's hand and reluctantly followed McHuish.

The bar was enclosed in an L-shaped alcove. The President of British Bank was recognized at once. A bevy of bankers encircled him, their restrained welcomes difficult to ignore. Dirk stood with Kim in the background, waiting for McHuish's lead.

'Look, Dirk . . .' He followed her eyes: around the corner, two lone figures were drinking at the bar.

He pressed her arm and calmly peered across to the other side of the room.

'Keep talking,' he murmured. 'Don't recognize them.'

He crossed with her to the bar, ordered a couple of beers, then joined McHuish's circle.

The President introduced them: 'Friends of mine; here on holiday.'

The conversation ebbed and flowed. It was several moments before Dirk detached McHuish.

'Over there, drinking by themselves,' he whispered. 'Sciacca and his girl-friend. While they're here, there's no danger.'

McHuish nodded. He sipped his Martini, inclined his head. 'Stick close to them, Trevallack. Don't lose them. I'll tell Freissiger to hold things.'

McHuish looked up, smiled sociably at Kim. As he turned back to his colleagues, he spoke softly to Dirk: 'Follow them wherever they go and . . .', he hesitated, before adding under his breath: 'Use your gun if you have to.'

At 12.25, the bankers, droves of them, were filing like sheep escaping the dipping pen, from the bar to the dining-room. At 12.34, several minutes after the last guest had disappeared, Sciacca and Erika rose from their bar-stools. Dirk passed Kim a fashion magazine from the marble wall-top.

Sciacca walked nonchalantly across the hall to the *garde robe*. He stooped down and picked up a large, orange-coloured case with an advertising motif stencilled on its side. He checked the contents, then slung the strap over his shoulder, while Erika waited for him. She stood in the centre of the hall, insolent, self-assured as she stared with boredom at the receptionist. She checked her watch against the grandfather clock.

'Quick, Kim, our skis.'

Dirk hustled her down the tiled staircase to the ski-room below. They grabbed their gear and rushed out into the open. Sciacca and his woman were already hailing one of the horse-drawn sledges. Strapping on his ski-bag and dragging on his mitts, Dirk approached the couple.

'Mind if we share the ride?' he asked.

'Where d'you want to go?' Sciacca asked brusquely. 'We're in a hurry.'

'To the village. Thanks.'

Sciacca turned his back, murmured something to his impatient woman. Dirk bundled Kim into the front seat and tucked the furs about their knees.

'It's clouding over,' Kim volunteered. 'Pity, after such a glorious morning.'

Erika's mouth curled at the corners. 'Skiing are you? Not lunching at the hotel?'

Dirk smiled indulgently. 'We like the pistes to ourselves.'

'Shouldn't go out now, if I was you,' the Sicilian snapped. 'Dangerous.'

'Meaning . . .?' Dirk slipped his hand into his anorak pocket.

'Another blizzard.'

The conversation ceased ten minutes later as the sledge drew up at the steps of the Krabach Kopf *seilbahn*. Sciacca paid off the driver and began to mount the steps. He rounded suddenly on Dirk: 'Stay here, if you know what's good for you,' the angry Sicilian snarled. He was pushing Erika up head of him. 'I dislike being followed, Herr Trevallack. Take the next car.' He hustled on and slapped two passes down on the lip of the pay desk.

'You've plenty of time, Herr Sciacca.'

Rudi Strauss was at the barrier. His jovial face was smiling as he recognized Dirk and Kim. 'D'you think I'd send the car up without you? Wendelin is doing the midday provisions run.' He took their tickets and passed them through the turnstile. 'The car is half-empty anyway.'

He moved to the doorway leading to his control-room. 'The weather is worsening,' he growled over his shoulder. 'Catch the next car down, if the visibility is bad. The wind's getting up.'

Chapter 22

Geiger was glowering impatiently at the doorway to the cabin.

'No room, Herr Dirk.' He pointed to the water-cans and the heap of cartons strewn about the floor. 'Next car, please.'

'Balls.'

Dirk shoved his way into the cabin. He pulled Kim after him and slammed the doors shut behind him. He looked up to the control-room where Rudi, grinning all over his face, waved them off. The car jerked, then swung off into space.

Nereo Sciacca stood in the leading corner of the cabin. A hatchet-faced man was helping him to lift the heavy radio from its bright orange case. The assistant erected the long, telescopic aerial.

Erika stood in the centre, between the water-cans, watching Kim. The third passenger was the big Arab who had been Sciacca's guest at the Farmers' Supper. He lounged against the windows, binoculars to his eyes as he watched the slopes below the Kreigerspitz.

None of them carried skis. They all seemed to know each other, but they spoke little as the cable-car lurched above the village. Geiger remained sullenly by the door, as Dirk steered Kim to the rear window. Peering through the perspex at the opposite side of the valley, he saw two men, black dots in the snow, at the head of the snowfields on either side of the gully.

The cabin was rattling across the lower pylon, its carrier wheels whining above their heads. Two minutes later, the village below was already a toy-town disappearing in the gloom. Dirk turned round, his mind racing.

The aerial on Sciacca's radio had been fully extended; the hatchet-man was pulling on his gloves to hold the heavy case. They were of red leather, the left hand marked with the insignia of the weather station; below it, in brackets, were the letters ZDK. His right-hand glove bore only the motif of the weather station.

The cabin was racing upwards at full speed. Dirk pushed Kim behind him, as he whipped out Rice's gun.

'Drop that transmitter, Sciacca,' he rapped. 'I'll kill you if you don't.'

The carrier wheels whirred above them. Erika backed away. Sciacca turned angrily. Khan grinned.

Nereo Sciacca lowered the transmitter, and slammed it back into the orange case.

'What the hell are you playing at?' he roared. 'You mad?'

'You've murdered Rice and you're holding his wife hostage. And . . .'

The red shadow of No. 1 car flashed past in the opposite direction, on its way from the summit. Dirk glanced at it – and in that fraction of time, the pistol was knocked from his hand.

Geiger sprang forwards, pinioning Dirk's arms. Khan picked up the gun. Erika retreated against the far-side doors. A miniature pistol was in her hand and levelled at Kim's stomach.

'Bravo, Wendelin,' Nereo snapped. 'Hold him until the job's done.'

The cliff below the Axe was racing up to meet them. The weather station was looming in sight. Sciacca was peering across at the opposite side of the valley. The hotel, a minuscule building, nestled in the snow below.

Sciacca lifted the orange-coloured case. He slapped it against the leading window. A brilliant light flickered from the farm (iodine quartz, Dirk guessed). Each occupant of the cabin turned to face the Kreigerspitz snowfields.

Puffs of white mist floated upwards, little mushroom clouds across the top of the snowfields. For several seconds they watched, each individual waiting for the nightmare they knew was to come. The hands on Kim's wristwatch showed 13.02.

Two hair-lines streaked horizontally across the crests of the snowfields. The mountainside began to move, slowly at first, and then the slabs broke away below the summit. Two misty clouds began rolling down the flanks of the mountains, two terrible outriders to the million tons of snow gathering momentum behind them.

Chapter 23

Donald McHuish slipped into his place on the right of this year's Director-General, the leading French banker presiding at the head of the VIPs' table.

'Teutonic thoroughness,' Gaston de Phalle murmured across to McHuish. 'Herr Freissiger is, as usual, on time to the minute. The Anglo-Saxons retain their liking for the theatrical.' The pendulum clock by the entrance to the dining-room was chiming the half-hour.

Franz Freissiger, his pale-faced wife beside him, stood in the door-way opening to the restaurant. As he began his speech, McHuish caught sight of the big Sicilian and his blonde sitting at the table in the other room. Trevallack must have remained in the lounge . . .

Freissiger, a dignified man in his dark green Austrian suit, wel-comed them, first in German, then in halting English. He spoke briefly, then moved across to the swing doors connecting the kitchen. They were flung open by the two attendant waitresses and there, standing dramatically in the centre, stood the hotel's chef, in white hat and chequered trousers. In his outstretched arms, he held high a silver platter from which a boar's head stared with unseeing eyes.

The chef marched into the dining-room. There was a burst of spontaneous clapping, and at that moment McHuish glimpsed two shadowy figures rising from their table in the restaurant behind Freissiger. The time, McHuish noted, was 12.34. He thought fast, restraining the urge to rise to his feet.

The chef was advancing down the length of the tables. Staid bankers, lounging back in their chairs, turned their heads and raised their schnapps in admiration. The boar's head came to rest at the end table where the carvers waited to carve.

McHuish caught de Phalle's eye.

'Donald,' Gaston murmured, leaning across the table, 'reply with a word of thanks, will you? I'm keeping my address of welcome until the cognac. Choose your moment.'

The President of British Bank demurred appropriately, then nodded modestly in agreement.

The waitresses, at a signal from the *maître d'hôtel*, approached the tables, the stacks of hot plates clattering as they were dispensed. Eight minutes had slipped by: it was already 12.42.

A waiter leaned over him discreetly, a green bottle of Moselle in his hand. Donald waited until his soup was served, then, nodding to the Director-General, he laid down his napkin. Apologizing to his neighbour, he pushed back his chair and rose from the table.

He felt all eyes were upon him as he threaded his way through the bustling servers. He noted the anxiety on Freissiger's face, as the Austrian came towards him. The clock chimed the three-quarters as they reached the door.

'Sciacca has gone,' Donald muttered. 'We've got to act fast. D'you agree, Herr Freissiger?'

The Austrian did not falter, though this crisis would cost him weeks of planning, waste tens of thousands of schillings.

'I'm with you,' he said quietly. 'Leave the details to me.' He snatched a tablespoon and rapped it against an empty soup tureen.

In the astonished sudden silence, McHuish heard the ticking of the clock behind him. He felt his heart thumping against his ribs. He would not, until the end of his days, forget this moment: 12.49.

'Director-General, ladies and gentlemen . . .' he began. Never before had he been forced to control his voice in the hundreds of speeches he had delivered. 'On your behalf, I must thank Herr Freissiger for this magnificent banquet. . . .' The chink of glasses, the bravos, the clapping would dull the pinic. 'But, ladies and gentlemen, I have something to say which you must accept at once, without question . . . *and without panic* . . .'

In the hush someone dropped a piece of cutlery. At the back, a group began murmuring and laughing amongst themselves.

'Please move fast, as soon as the proprietor tells you what to do, where to go. We must evacuate this room and the hotel *at once*. There is imminent danger of an avalanche in the valley. Please, remain calm, listen to the proprietor's instructions and – above all – *no* panic.'

He stood back to allow Freissiger to have his say. The clock was ticking remorselessly behind him: 12.53.

The Austrian's clipped words passed over Donald's head, as he stared through the windows to the greying sky outside. The snow-fields had lost their glare and he could see the flags of the ski-school hut flapping in the wind.

'. . . and now, ladies and gentlemen,' Freissiger was saying, 'our guests at the tables nearest this doorway will leave first. Our staff will direct you down to our underground swimming-pool . . . hurry, please, in silence and there will be no danger.'

He smiled serenely, nodded to the guests at the table on his right. There was an embarrassed laugh and then the exodus began: 12.57.

McHuish stood by Freissiger's side while the room emptied. There was no panic, no unpleasantness. When the last guest reached the hall, the kitchen team and the domestic staff followed with good-humoured discipline. As Frau Freissiger, Franz and McHuish brought up the rear, the hands of the clock in the hallway had just passed one o'clock . . .

McHuish had walked by the attractive sledge, so tastefully decorated with dried summer flowers, when he spotted the mask of the stuffed fox snarling at him from the low wall in the alcove. Those glazed, tormented eyes would remain in his memory for the rest of his days. At that moment, he heard a low rumble, like gun-fire, too reminiscent of Alamein. The noise became louder, increased to a thunderous roar. There was a whistling sound and the slamming of shutters outside . . . and then he felt the pressure on his ears. He cried out in pain as the shock-wave slammed the building – he began running after Freissiger who was hurrying down the stairway lead- ing to the pool.

Chapter 24

The whirr of the suspension wheels was the only sound. Each inmate of the cable-car stood speechless, mesmerized by the horror on the opposite side of the valley.

'*Mein Gott!*' Erika, her fingers to her lips, broke the silence. Then they heard it, the growing rumble that grew into a deafening roar.

Geiger relaxed his grip. Dirk shook himself free; grabbed Kim, held her close, as they watched the avalanche plunging down upon the unsuspecting hotel . . .

The twin demons barely moved at first – then, as the snow clouds billowed upwards, rolling ahead of the advancing snow, the centres of the avalanches began to converge. Sweeping onwards and gathering momentum, they plunged into the gully above the hotel.

The first waves struck the opposite cliffs, exploded, bounced backwards and upwards. The spiralling clouds of snow-filled air sprang high, billowing outwards and down, deep into the valley. The hotel vanished, overwhelmed by millions of tons of snow and rocks.

The airborne monster was now licking across the valley, travelling at terrifying speed, devouring everything: trees, rocks, buildings – all had disappeared beneath this irresistible holocaust that was fanning across the valley floor. Swirling upwards and generating its own typhoon, the shock-wave suddenly struck the cliffs below the Krabach Kopf.

The trees were the first to vanish, their tops snapping off like matchsticks. Then the mushroom tops of the snow-filled clouds leaped upwards towards the Axe.

He choked, gasping for air as the shock-wave struck them. He felt an excruciating pain in his lungs, heard the women screaming. The cabin heaved, then flung outwards. The Axe was rearing towards them, advancing to smash them to atoms. As he watched, gripping the rails with all his strength, the pylon jerked suddenly then slowly toppled towards them . . .

The water-cans crashed against the sides. Kim screamed. Sciacca swore. Erika fell – and then they were all struggling on the cabin floor which was sliding away beneath their feet. As Dirk looked upwards, he glimpsed the Axe pylon twisting suddenly, as if crushed in a giant's hand. The steel erection tipped; the suspension cable of No. 2 jerked free from its guides – and then the red painted steelwork was leaning precariously over the canyon yawning beneath them.

He never knew what happened next, only that the bottom was slipping out of their world. A door crashed open as the cabin bounced. Geiger yelled as a stack of cartons plummeted into the void outside – and then the car was falling away, gathering speed as it plunged downwards along its suspension cable . . .

The shrieking of the wind was worse than the tortuous scream of the wires – and, as Dirk closed his eyes to shut out oblivion, the cabin slowed, then jerked to a halt.

He heard Erika whimpering in the corner. He caught hold of Kim, silent and white. He clung to the rail, waiting for the swinging to cease. And then he knew they were alive, hanging by a thread, hundreds of metres above the Schreck valley. Geiger was scrambling to his feet and trying to reach the telephone.

Suddenly there was no sound, nothing but the whining of the wind outside.

Chapter 25

Rudi Strauss watched No. 2 car disappearing into the murk. He tapped his aneroid barometer, glanced through his control room window to the cloud sweeping across the Krabach Kopf.

This would be the last trip. He would close the lifts, as soon as he had lowered No. 2 again. With his left hand he picked up the phone to the restaurant at the summit. With his right, he reached for the pencil to make up his one o'clock log.

'That you, Hans?'

'*Ja.*'

'Wind's getting up. I'll wait till you're ready. Hurry, if you want to get down tonight.'

He hung up, laughed at the obscenities which his old friend flung down at him from the summit. He glanced at the distance metre: No. 1 would be crossing the Axe in a few seconds; he slowed the control, reduced the rate of descent. He waited the prescribed twenty seconds, then built up the speed again. He would not object to shutting-up earlier tonight.

Those foreigners from the weather station were an arrogant, obnoxious lot – that big brute, Nereo Sciacca seemed to consider he owned Schreck. He, Rudi Strauss, had certainly called their bluff when he had kept the car waiting for the English couple. With a flourish, he pencilled his initials across the 13.00 column of the log.

'What's up, Tania, girl?' He often talked to his brown and white spaniel bitch who accompanied him on his watches. She shared the long hours, understood his moods. He allowed her to lick his hand as she came up to him whining, her tail between her legs.

'Thunder again?'

She was terrified of storms – and then he heard it, the rumble up the valley. He was right to close the lifts.

He glanced through the wide, plate-glass window. No. 1 should be emerging from the murk – but, God, what was that, that terrible whistling note, that roar that was filling the valley? A *lawine* – nothing else could generate this overwhelming sound.

He glanced through the side window – both the Kreigerspitz

snowfields were snowballing into a gigantic cloud of white mist. In a convoluting, steam-rolling motion, the *lawine* disappeared suddenly behind the hills hiding the Schreckhorn Hotel.

The wind blast struck next, a fierce gust that jerked the needles of his anemometer against the stops. He felt the shock-wave, gasped as his lungs compressed. He turned to watch the hauling cable swinging while the cars continued their trips . . .

'Thank God.'

There was No. 1 clear of the Axe now. He could just distinguish the red pylon, with No. 2 almost up to it . . .

A second shock struck suddenly, squeezing the breath from his body. He cried out, then saw the incredible happen . . .

The Axe pylon was toppling, slowly at first, then with a lurch. It halted suddenly to lean grotesquely over the cliff. He reached for the emergency brake: grabbed it, heaved with all his strength.

There was nothing to do but watch. Mesmerized, he saw No. 1 sliding down, gathering momentum before the electro-magnets checked the speed. The car slid to a halt, barely a hundred metres from the station.

No. 2 had stopped, swinging on its cable, when the wire jumped the Axe. But now it was plunging headlong in the cable loop that was oscillating rhythmically across the valley line. The automatics could never brake that descent – everything depended on the cable, on the pylon—'*Oh, God* . . .' and he cried out as the minuscule cabin jerked like a marionette in the wind.

He was trembling when finally he let go of the brake. No. 2 was just visible, lolling in the bight of the cable below the cliff: the car had come to rest some three hundred metres from the rocks.

The faint tinkle of the cabin telephone brought him to his senses. A far-away voice, barely intelligible in the crackling atmosphere, was recognizable as Geiger's.

'That you, Strauss?'

'Yes. What's the state of things?'

'All alive. Can you hear me okay?'

'Just.'

'We're trying to sort ourselves out. I'll phone you back . . .'

'Emergency procedure, Geiger. Stick to the drill.'

He heard the bitter laughter, then Geiger spoke again: 'It's bloody cold up here. It'll soon be dark.'

'Hold on. Wait for orders.'

Rudi Strauss hung up, then grabbed the outside phone: 'Police,' he shouted at the operator. 'Police.'

The phone clicked as the policeman's wife came on the line: '*Ursula*,' he shouted. 'Where's Stefan? Accident on the Krabach Kopf *seilbahn*.'

'He's out on the black run, below the Krabach Kopf, searching for a body.'

'Listen carefully, Ursula, get through to town. Report the accident and tell 'em there's a full emergency on here. Call out all the services, d'you understand? There's been a *lawine* up the valley. Hurry, for God's sake, Ursula . . .'

He hung up, opened the door and yelled down the stairs to his wife. She'd have to run for help. With luck and with the utmost care, he might be able to lower No. 1 down before dark.

He glanced outside and swore. The wind was getting up and the first flakes were falling.

Chapter 26

The time by Dirk's watch was 4.20. Pin-points of light were weaving like glow-worms, hundreds of metres below the swaying cabin where the rescue teams gathered in the last moments of daylight.

Geiger, crouched in his corner, was still in contact on his phone with the *seilbahn*, but communications seemed difficult. Strauss had somehow managed to lower No. 1 cabin to the bottom pylon. The commander of the rescue team was at his side: the orders that now crackled over the phone were concise and confident.

In spite of the catastrophic disaster higher up the valley, Strauss had somehow mounted a rescue attempt on the cable-car. 'Hang on and keep warm,' had been the last intelligible command . . .' and then the line had died.

The accident to No. 2 cabin had brought a strange cohesion to the shocked occupants. The instinct of self-preservation had submerged the hostilities and the divisions which would destroy them all. Nereo Sciacca, by mutual, unspoken consent, had assumed command – and Dirk, powerless now to influence events, was content for the Sicilian to have his way.

A cross-wind was buffeting the cabin and causing it to sway and jerk, like a puppet on a string. The motion was nauseous and Kim had been sick in the corner. Dirk, his back to the rear corner, was trying to comfort her against his shoulder, but the stench was unsettling them all.

Erika had become hysterical and was shouting obscenities at the only other member of her sex, but a savage slap across the face from Nereo jerked her to her senses. Her whimpering from the opposite corner was straining all their nerves. Zydek was standing by his master; he had remained silent throughout the whole ordeal.

Khan heard it first, the sudden fluttering above the crescendo of the wind. He jumped to his feet as two lights flared in the dusk to windward of the cabin. Against their glare, Dirk picked out the loom of a helicopter hovering above them, its rotors flashing above the lights.

All seven passengers were on their feet, peering through the perspex windows. As the chopper hung there, Dirk could see the white-helmeted pilot, his face half-turned in concentration as he judged his drift. He made his decision and down swooped the machine, barely ten metres clear.

'Quick,' Sciacca yelled. 'Erika and you.' He stabbed a finger at Kim. 'Up through the roof. . . . Khan, open the hatch.'

The big Arab needed no prompting. He had jerked the aluminium ladder from its rest and was shinning up its rungs to the rectangular door in the roof. A blast of icy air exploded in the cabin as he clambered through the hatch.

Erika went first, shoved from below as the cage, dangling on the end of the chopper's wire, scraped the roof of the cabin. Her screams were carried away in the wind as she was pulled by Khan towards the latticed grille. And then she was away, dangling in the void like a yo-yo as the wire hauled her upwards into the belly of the hovering machine.

'You're next, Kim . . .'

He squeezed her hand and thrust her on to the rungs of the ladder. The cage swung down again; Khan heaved her through the hatch, then clung to her on the icy, heaving roof. The wire slapped across the cabin. Then she was safely inside the cage and swinging into space.

'*My God, look at Khan* . . .' shouted Sciacca.

In the pool of light below the chopper, the cage was dancing crazily. It swung like a pendulum, at long span, beneath the gleaming belly of the chopper . . . and clawing like a spider to the latticework was the spread-eagled figure of the Arab.

The chopper drew away, gradually losing height. As it was disappearing in the gloom, the cage flicked suddenly. The spiderman was flung clear, his legs thrashing as he vanished into the void.

The twin lights of the helicopter, faint blurs now, checked their descent, stabilized, then slowly gained height as the machine disappeared into the darkening night.

Chapter 27

By six o'clock, a blizzard was raging. The lights on the valley floor were obliterated and the wind was pounding on the walls of the cabin. The four survivors had to shout to make themselves heard, as the cold began to destroy their resistance: they had wasted too much energy replacing the upper hatch.

At 6.12, Geiger's telephone call lamp flickered. He grabbed the instrument from its socket, shouted incoherently into the mouthpiece, then slammed it back into its rest.

'They've manœuvred the emergency cage over the Axe,' he yelled. 'It's on its way down to us.' He was staring at Sciacca. 'It takes four, including the operator. There are only four men left at the summit. The Axe pylon is damaged, so they'll lift only two of us on this next trip. They insist that I should be one of them, so that I can help.'

No one spoke as Geiger continued excitedly:

'I didn't ask for this: the cage has to be wound back again uphill by hand, if the petrol engine fails to work.'

Sciacca was watching Dirk, each reading the other's thoughts.

'Why don't I shoot you, Trevallack?' the Sicilian snarled. 'And Geiger – or Zydek? Only one more lift, and I'd be safe.'

'For the gallows?' Dirk snapped. 'They may not know you sprang the avalanche, but the chopper crew have seen us all.'

Dirk grinned to hide his fear. 'You'll have to choose, Sciacca, who's next. D'you think the last two will survive the night?'

They were all watching him, the big Sicilian with the flashing eyes. Zydek, morose, imperturbable; Geiger, impatient, terrified . . . and Dirk? He knew he was in Sciacca's power. Even if Dirk could turn the tables and retrieve the gun, what would that gain now? 'You're a cold-blooded murderer, Sciacca. If you survive this, they'll string you up.'

A blow across the face sent Dirk reeling into the corner. He wiped the blood from the corner of his mouth, saw Zydek's grin. And, at that instant, a light flickered in the darkness, a yellow glow, above the leading window. The outline of a steel cage was edging towards them and then there was a scratching against the metal body of the cable-car.

'*Zydek* . . .' Sciacca pointed at the silent man, then slid back a leeward door. He grabbed Geiger's arm. '*And you, you bastard. . . .*' He shoved the younger man towards the gaping rectangle. 'If you open your mouths about the avalanche, I'll drag you in too.'

The snow-flakes curled inside, when Geiger flung back the other door. He waited until the cage jolted alongside, judged his moment, then stepped out into the night. An instant later, a pair of gloved hands reached inside. Grabbing them, Zydek placed a foot on the lip of the swaying cage and jumped. A voice shouted above the wind. Dirk edged to the door, as a package and a coil of rope were flung into the cabin. The cylindrical lattice-work crept slowly upwards, then disappeared into the blizzard. Sciacca slammed shut the doors.

'If they can get over the pylon,' he shouted, 'it's our turn next.' He turned upon Dirk, a smirk on his twisted face.

'And if they'll take only one of us next time, Trevallack, I don't give much for your chances.'

Dirk did not bother to reply. He peered at his watch; the phosphorous on the hands was indistinct, but the time *could* be 7.10. The cold was eating into him. He stamped his feet and shivered in the darkness.

They had not spoken, it seemed, for a long while. Dirk felt drowsy, though they had taken turns in striding to and fro across the restricted floor space. Sciacca remained silent with this thoughts.

The upward haul of the rescue cage; the negotiation of the crumpled pylon in the blizzard and the darkness; all this frenzied work under impossible conditions *must* take several hours. The cage would have to slide down again, across the Axe and feel its way to the stricken cabin. Their rescuers could not possibly return before 9.30 or 10.00.

To remain alive in this bitter cold was their only concern. They would never survive the night, though the stores that had been hauled through the door would postpone the final agony. Two vacuum flasks of hot soup, slabs of chocolate, two loaves of rye bread and salami – Sciacca and he had swallowed one flask and were saving the second until later. They would ration the food throughout the night, if the cage did not reappear. Sciacca had tossed the package across to Dirk, for him to open – the first evidence of humanity that Sciacca had shown.

Kim, his beloved girl – had she reached ground safely? A cool customer, that chopper pilot – he had only just made it before the night clamped in . . . but, in the silence of their waiting, Dirk felt that death was breathing down their necks.

The cold was freezing his blood and it was an effort to think . . . it was an effort trying to decipher the hands on his watch – but it was at least past 10.30. . . . The rescuers had abandoned the attempt – why risk further life, having saved the majority? And what of the victims down in the Schreckhorn valley, twisted out of recognition, battered to bits, suffocated by Sciacca's avalanche?

'Trevallack . . .?'

'Yes.'

'D'you see something there?'

Dirk peered through the iced-up front window. A light was swaying there, flickering in their crazy, disorientated world . . .

Slowly the cage came into focus. He dared not trust his eyes as they hauled themselves to their feet. They clutched the handrails to prevent themselves from being hurled about as the cabin tossed in the storm. The cage crashed alongside the front panel, scraping at the perspex.

For an interminable moment, nothing happened. Then there was a tapping on the window and a shout being carried away on the wind . . .

'We're jammed together,' Sciacca shouted. 'He can't free the cage.'

They scraped away a patch of ice from the window. The operator of the cage, enveloped in his bulky survival suit, was trying to lever the cage from the invisible projection of the cabin. He was yanking at the handle of the winch, to free the cage by hauling it upwards again. The wire was taut and thrumming in the wind.

The cabin trembled. There was a metallic crash, as if there had been an explosion – and then the cage suddenly fell away, disappearing into the blackness of the night.

Sciacca yelled as their world disintegrated, the cabin slipping away beneath their feet.

'For Christ's sake, hold on,' Dirk yelled in the darkness, as the cabin gained momentum. The suspension wheels screamed, the cable whined and the wind began tearing at their lungs.

Down, down into the blackness, twisting, falling, hurled against the sides of their aluminium box. He shut his eyes, waiting for oblivion – and then he knew no more.

Chapter 28

Nereo Sciacca had lain in the darkness for he knew not how long. He was disorientated, but gradually his world drifted back into focus – and then he felt the pain throbbing in his ankle.

He was alive – and still in this bucketing cable-car . . . the gusts of the blizzard were buffeting continually against the side and the infernal thing was swinging like a pendulum. But where was it, how far had it fallen? How high was he above the valley? And then he remembered the Englishman . . .

The pendulum motion was battering the steel water-drums against each other in a maddening cacophony. The floor of the cabin was sheet ice from the spilled and frozen water. His gloves stuck to the floor – and then he heard the groan from the opposite corner of the cabin.

He crawled across the floor, felt in the darkness for the other man. His fingers traced the outline of the face.

'Trevallack,' he shouted above the wind. 'Trevallack. Wake up.'

If he was alive, he'd respond – and he crooked his fore-arm beneath the neck. He dragged the body across the floor, propped the shoulder against the side.

'For God's sake, man, come to your senses . . .' and he slapped the chilled face. If Trevallack was to die now, he, Nereo Sciacca, stood no chance – together they might exist. While there was breath, there was life . . . and so long as life remained, there was still the chance they could survive this interminable, hellish night. He pummelled the man's chest, yelled into the night, his words obscene, dragged from the gutters of his past.

'For Christ's sake . . .' The Englishman's words were slurred as he tried to haul himself to his feet. 'What time is it? Where the hell are we?'

Painfully, feeling their way and instinctively making allowances for the other, they began to fight again for survival. They were alive. The cable-car had not torn adrift. The night must, in the end, drag into dawn.

'My watch is smashed,' Sciacca growled. 'Give me your wrist.'

He took Trevallack's arm, felt the cold of his flesh. '10.50.'

'Eight hours till dawn,' the Englishman said. His teeth were chattering but he had gained his feet and was hanging to the rail. 'Any more soup left?'

Sciacca found the carton, felt the roundness of the vacuum flask, shook it to his ear. The broken glass tinkled in the container.

'It'll be cold,' he said. 'Bread and sausage?'

He felt for the bread, found the meat. Together they chewed the food in the darkness. Despair retreated and they began to plan, searching for some way out.

'We've dropped a long way,' Trevallack said. He detested hanging in space like this – he felt as if he was falling through the floor. He shivered again, stamped his feet. 'We've got to retain our core heat – keep moving, that's our only chance.' He laughed bitterly. 'That's what they taught us in the Royals.'

Sciacca did not bother to ask for an explanation. The cold was killing them both. The icy finger of death was upon them – and rational thought was becoming more and more difficult. His body ached for sleep – to stretch himself out, never to wake again – how simple a way out. He allowed his legs to buckle and slithered to the frozen floor.

Dirk never knew how long his loathsome companion had lain there in the darkness. His own brain was slowly freezing up and reasoned thought was now too difficult. Then he realized that, without Sciacca, he himself could not last long.

'Nereo,' he yelled. 'Sciacca, keep awake, you bloody murderer.' He kicked the prostrate body and felt it stir. He reached down and tried to haul the man to his feet. Then he collapsed himself, his strength ebbing in the freezing cold. Sciacca was groping in the darkness. His arms locked suddenly about Dirk's chest.

In repugnance, Dirk struck out. But suddenly he felt the warmth of the other man. He reached out too and together they lay there, giving to each the warmth of the other.

'Where d'you come from?' Sciacca asked.

'Cornwall . . . born in St Ives, west of England.'

Dirk smelt the garlic on the man's breath. 'You're from Sicily, aren't you?'

'Yes. Trapani. My father was a fisherman. I helped him with the mullet.'

Then in this darkened world, hanging high in the blizzard whirling about them, the two men from alien worlds slumped down to wait for the inevitable. The big Sicilian shivered and began to weep.

Dirk felt his own strength slowly ebbing, but, as he closed his eyes, Nereo Sciacca began to talk. He spoke slowly, the words tumbling from him. He spoke of his childhood in Trapani; his youth; his broken marriage, and finally, how the Mafia had been the easiest way out of his mess.

'D'you regret it now?' Dirk asked. 'Yours is the responsibility, but not perhaps the fault.' His words sounded pretentious; he wished he'd never spoken.

'I've killed men. Blackmailed, cheated, tortured . . . and you ask if I regret it?' The hoarse sobs racked his body, as he clung like a child in the darkness.

'Have *you* not sinned, Englishman? You, with your different style of life, are you proud of all you've done?'

A fiercer gust than most slammed against the cabin. The cable trembled overhead.

'Are you frightened of death?' Dirk asked. 'You, Nereo, who's killed so callously, are you afraid to die?'

In the silence, Dirk heard the man's breathing slowly regaining its rhythm.

'I've never considered the matter until now. If there was a priest, I'd confess my sins. I'd be ready then – at peace, I think, before I go.'

'D'you need a priest? Is he vital to your faith?'

'That was my religion – when once I had one.'

'For me, it's God and I, no one in between.'

'That's simple for you, then. Too easy perhaps.'

'Belief is what you learn through the tragedies of life. Not what they tell you. You have to find out for yourself.'

'That's too easy, too. In my religion, the one I had, you can't evade the rules. Mortal sin damns your soul. And that means hell, Englishman . . .'

He spoke calmly, with a humility that had not been there before.

'I've never cared much about my soul till now. I've killed. I've murdered men and women in that avalanche. I deserve to die – and even if we could survive these next few hours, they'll take my life.'

'There's no capital punishment in Austria,' Dirk said. 'You'd spend your life behind bars.'

'I'd sooner die than that.'

Sciacca lay still then. Then he continued, talking to himself.

'Does it matter to you, Trevallack, what you believe?'

Dirk searched deeply before answering. Strange, how easily the words came with death so very close . . .

'Yes, it does. I have my sins, too. I've confessed them only once to a clergyman. A sort of insurance, I suppose.'

'So why confess, if that was all?' The Sicilian spoke without rancour, without condemnation. 'To justify confession, presupposes forgiveness.' He was speaking quietly, his words almost inaudible: '. . . and who can forgive, Englishman?'

They lay there in the darkness, drawing strength and warmth from each other, the murderer and the bank employee. Minutes passed before Dirk replied: 'We've had all our lives in which to live a faith,' he said. 'Do we need the imminence of death really to know His truth?'

'He knew what it was to die.'

'For the likes of us?'

'Even us.'

The blizzard howled outside. Sciacca lay silent, growing colder, moving little . . . but when he spoke again, his voice was firm: 'D'you hear me, Englishman?'

'Yes, Nereo.'

'Jesus Christ. D'you believe in Him?'

'Yes. He's very close.'

'Listen to me, witness this. I'm asking Him to forgive my lousy life.'

Dirk lay still. The snow-flakes hissed against the windows, but the motion of the cabin seemed steadier, more regular with its swing.

'Sciacca . . .?'

'You heard me?'

'Yes. Now do the same for me.'

The cold was overwhelming them at last. He closed his eyes, ready to die. He'd had his fill of happiness, compared to most. And Kim was safe – she'd have his child perhaps. 'Forgive me, Lord,' he prayed. 'Forgive us both – and our Sicilian here.' As he opened his eyes for what must be the last time, Sciacca gripped his arm.

'D'you notice anything, Englishman?'

Dirk tried to raise his head to listen. He felt so weak, his limbs useless, numb. Then slowly he realized that the wind had died. The flutter of falling snow was the only sound.

They helped one another, dragging each other upright. Then he tripped and fell, his foot through the coil of rope lying between the water-cans.

Chapter 29

'If I die, you die,' Trevallack said.

They had scraped away a patch of frost from the leeward window. The snow was still falling but the cold was more bearable, now that the wind had eased.

'If we just sit here, we'll both die,' Sciacca retorted. 'If you're prepared to risk your neck for both of us, I'll help you. If you never reach the bottom, I'll die, anyway, so what would be the point of my killing you?' He smiled sardonically. 'If we succeed with your harebrained scheme, at the worst for me it's imprisonment for life.'

Their activity gave them strength. Dirk fingered through his ski-bag and extracted a handful of karabiner shackles, while Nereo coiled the thin, nylon rope. 'If it will hold you,' the Sicilian said, 'it'll be strong enough for me.'

'If you lose your end of the rope, Nereo, you lose your life. You know that, don't you?'

Sciacca nodded, but he was not listening as he peered long through the back window.

'Down there, Trevallack. . . I thought I saw a light.' They glared through the darkness.

'You're seeing things. The snow's letting up, but we're too far up the lift to see the ground, let alone the bottom pylon. When the Axe collapsed, we fell vertically, in the bight of the cable.'

'Hope you're bloody well wrong. You've got to reach the lower pylon . . .'

'Two chances, haven't we? But if I reach the bottom, you've got to be quick, Nereo. Haul up as fast as you can.'

'And don't forget the schnapps . . .'

Though the snow had stopped, each knew that their chances were practically nil; their sole consolation was that the risk was worth the odds. They worked sluggishly, forcing their brains to function, trying to beat the onset of exposure.

'All set,' Dirk asked. 'For God's sake, take a turn with the bare end when I've gone.'

He hitched up the ladder and climbed to the hatchway.

The plate was frozen into its rectangle. He felt for the knife in his ski-bag and began jabbing at the hatch-combing. Sciacca wrenched the knife from him, firmly removed him from the ladder, then finished the job.

Dirk remounted again, after handing the karabiners to Sciacca. He extracted his own length of nylon from his ski-bag and tied a bowline beneath his arm-pits.

'Pass me the shackles, one at a time . . .'

He threw down the hatch and scrambled on to the roof. He felt no vertigo, no terror as he clambered in the darkness, swinging between life and extinction. One arm crooked about the cable, he carefully shackled a necklace together with five of the clips; with the sixth, he completed the circle around the suspension wire.

'Pass up my end. . .'

He threaded the rope's end through a sheave on the suspension rollers, then passed it through the lowest karabiner of the necklace. He pulled up some slack, then carefully rove the clove-hitch on the bight. He threaded through the end and overhauled two metres of rope.

'Hand up a water-can.'

The metal container rattled against the hatchway. Sciacca supported its weight as Trevallack secured the end of the rope to its handle. Finally, Dirk passed the end of the bowline of his own lighter rope through the second lowest of his *abseil* karabiners. He over-hauled the slack and, with a round-turn and two half-hitches, secured his end around his wrist. Coiling up the remainder, he slipped it back into his ski-bag. He thrust his left leg into the water-can and took the weight on his bowline.

'Ready, Nereo?'

Sciacca was down in the cabin and shouting through the hatch-way.

'Down there, through the mist, *look* . . .'

Through the gap in the drifting cloud, Trevallack glimpsed a blur of yellow lights – and in that pool of incandescence he could see the midget figures of several men. They were clustered about the base of the lower pylon which supported the weight of the suspension cable, a hundred metres above the Strauss's *seilbahn*.

'We can't be more than two hundred metres from the pylon,' Dirk yelled down through the hatch. 'Our rope might just reach.' He stamped with his free leg on the aluminium roof. 'We've got a chance, Nereo,' he yelled into the night. 'Get a move on man. For God's sake, hurry . . .'

The mist rolled across again, shutting out the gap. The snow began falling and the lights vanished.

Sciacca was shouting through the hole in the cabin roof. 'Ready. I've got the weight.'

'Let me go. Four tugs on the rope from me and you haul back. Two, and you let the rope out. Understand?'

The last glimpse Trevallack had of the Sicilian was the outline of the huge head poking through the hatch. Trevallack took the weight on his personal bowline and slid his leg into the water-can. He slid over the lip of the cabin and dropped into the abyss.

He dangled there, swinging slowly from the cable, his weight taken by the container. He fought back the terror, refusing to think. Get down, start moving, you haven't much time, you stupid bugger. He jerked the can to start the slide – slowly at first, then, gathering speed, it shifted ever downwards, the karabiners screaming above him, screeching along the metal of the cable.

Sciacca was holding on, tightly checking the cradle from running out of control. The snow was driving thickly again, straight into his face, shutting out the world. He could feel the thick blackness of the night. He had no hands and the muscles in his arms were cramping up, and then the agony from his leg in the water-can became unbearable.

Swap my legs across – but I can't until the slide has eased. And when it has, will I be near enough to reach the pylon? They'll hear me if I yell, please God, they'll hear me? How much more rope, how much? I can't go on . . . his grip was weakening on the cable. And when he passed out, would he fall from the water-can, dangle in his bowline until he became frozen meat? He'd hang there, an iced-up corpse, swinging in the night.

The wind shrieked as he rushed headlong downwards, the cold tearing at his lungs. Then, as the speed of his descent slowed suddenly the rope jerked bar-taut.

He was swinging to and fro, a marionette, disconnected from the world. He cried out in panic, his cries carried away in the night.

'God, oh Jesus . . .'

So near was he, so close must he be to the pylon. With his ebbing strength he gave two savage tugs: when there was no response, he tugged again . . . but, if Nereo let him go, he too was lost.

150

Trevallack knew he had little time before exposure overtook him. He could not reason now, though he tried to force his brain. The cold was eating through him, freezing his senses. If he hung here, he would be dead in minutes . . . but succour and survival could not be far away. Whatever else, Sciacca must not haul back upon the rope.

He fumbled through his ski-bag with his left hand. His fingers closed on the cold steel of his knife. All he needed was another bowline, a bowline-on-the-bight around the cable, clear of the karabiners. And with his failing strength he tied it, the loop around the wire, to take his weight.

He overhauled the remainder of his rope, let it drop beneath him. Then, just as he was running out of line, he could feel the end touching the ground below. He could not be more than twenty metres above the snow . . .

He hesitated, his mind clearing suddenly. If he cut himself free, he would slide down the cable to the pylon; to smash against it was a risk he would have to take. If he survived, he could climb down and look for help.

His rope's tail was touching the snow, somewhere in the night. One of the rescue team he had seen might find it – and they would pull on the line; realize, when Sciacca replied, that life still flickered in the invisible cabin. They would send up food, hot drinks, and another life-line. They would rescue that strange, Sicilian murderer.

He wriggled his paralysed leg from the water-can. He gasped as his chest was crushed by his bowline. He slashed with his knife at the original sling . . .

He was rushing through the darkness, the freezing air clawing at his throat – ever downwards he tumbled, down into the abyss, his limbs jerking spasmodically in his sling. There was a roaring about his ears. As he slid slowly to a halt, a red mist swam before his eyes and suddenly there was peace.

In the early hours of Thursday 29 January, the second-in-command of the rescue section on the Krabach Kopf lift was returning to his home. He had left the others to finish off returning the equipment to the shelter beneath the *seilbahn*. He was taking the short-cut across the bottom of the valley when something slashed across his face. A rope hanging vertically, frozen as stiff as a steel cable, had sliced his cheek.

They brought down Nereo Sciacca alive. They had to amputate his foot. Six weeks afterwards, they charged him and Zydek with the murder of Antony Rice. If this police prosecution had failed, they would have re-arrested Sciacca and charged him with the murder of Klaus Foch, the handyman of the Schreckhorn Hotel. He was one of the three to be killed by the avalanche. The other two casualties were foresters. The 214 guests and staff had reached the safety of the underground swimming-pool before the avalanche demolished the hotel and overwhelmed the valley.

Nereo Sciacca was sentenced to imprisonment for life.

Epilogue

They found Dirk at dawn. He had been unable to haul himself up the last few metres of the cable which, for the final stretch, inclined upwards to the head of the first pylon.

His body was frozen stiff and they had to cut him down. They buried him in the little walled churchyard of Schreck. They named the new road to the Schreckhorn Hotel after him: *Trevallackstrasse*.

In January each year I make my pilgrimage. I visit the churchyard in Schreck. Afterwards, I take the train to the State's top security prison.

The last time I saw him, Sciacca was a changed man; he was philosophically facing his hopeless future. He helped me reconstruct the last terrible hours. He told me that more important than his life, he owed his peace of mind (and his soul, he said) to 'the Englishman'.

The prison chaplain asked to see me when I was there last year. Nereo Sciacca, he told me, was devoting the time left to him to helping others in the prison: the despairing, the hopeless, the embittered men.

The pain has eased. I shall not return again.

KQ